THE MAGIC INKSTAND AND OTHER STORIES

Heinrich Seidel

THE MAGIC INKSTAND

and other stories

Translated from the German by
Elizabeth Watson Taylor

Illustrated by
Wayne Anderson

JONATHAN CAPE
THIRTY BEDFORD SQUARE LONDON

This edition first published 1982

Jonathan Cape Ltd, 30 Bedford Square, London WC1

The stories first appeared in *Wintermärchen* by Heinrich Seidel, published in German in 1885

British Library Cataloguing in Publication Data

Seidel, Heinrich
[Wintermärchen. English].
The magic inkstand, and other stories.
I. Title II. The magic inkstand, and other stories
833'.8 PZ8
ISBN 0-224-01856-6

Typeset by Inforum Ltd, Portsmouth
Printed in Italy by New Interlitho SpA, Milan

To Annette,

who introduced me to these stories

E.W.T.

Contents

The Water Monster 9

The Dwarf Wood 25

The Cairn 43

The Christmas Country 50

The Snake-King 69

The Three Sisters 77

The Timepiece 87

Little Marie 96

Erica 112

The Wizard 131

The Magic Inkstand 149

The Water Monster

IN NORTHERN Germany there are great lakes full of coves and inlets which stretch between wooded hills, and are charmingly adorned with green islands. On such a lake, just at the spot where a stream joined it after flowing through green meadows and rustling beech-woods, a village lay in a wooded hollow, looking very much like an island itself, lying with its fields and meadows among the surrounding trees. In this village, quite near the water, a fisherman lived with his wife and small son whose name was Conrad. A little girl called Gertrude, the child of a neighbouring peasant, was Conrad's favourite playfellow. As their parents' gardens lay side by side, the children met every day, slipping from one to the other through a hole in the hedge; and each of them was as much at home in the next-door house as in his own. They also roamed together along the shores of the lake; it had many quiet, calm inlets, some covered in white water-lilies, others surrounded by reed-beds in which the black moorhen or the clumsy coot built their nests, and the tiny reed-warblers kept up their continuous, babbling song. In some places the shore was sandy, and open to the wash of waves. Here they looked for shells and stones, and collected all their treasures in a hiding-place between thorn-bushes where there was a small hollow in the clayey slope. There they had stored big shells shaped like mussels and all lined with mother-of-pearl, and stones that were as clear as glass or white like milk. Some were veined in bright colours, and one, which they particularly treasured, was transparent and, if you held it up to the light, it shone red like the sunrise.

They had some amber-coloured "thunder-stones" too; Conrad's grandmother had given this name to belemnite, because she said that it came from the sky in the lightning. But their greatest treasure was a smoothly polished stone axe-hammer such as our pagan ancestors used before the discovery of iron. The children had found it on a neighbouring island where Conrad's father sometimes took them with him when he went fishing. The island was thickly overgrown with big trees and low bushes and scrub, and was said to have been a shrine in pagan times; and at its highest point, under dark, age-old oak-trees, there actually were a number of great, moss-covered blocks of stone arranged in a circle. Once Conrad and Gertrude had penetrated the thicket that surrounded the place, but it was so gloomy and lonely there, with no sound but the whistling of the wind in the branches and the loud, unpleasant caw of a raven whose nest was in the oak-tree that, shuddering, the children hurried back to the lake-shore, where friendly sunshine and shining wavelets welcomed them.

As winter approached, other forms of entertainment were open to them. Sometimes there were long periods of extreme cold during which no snow fell. It was then that the entire lake became covered in a glassy sheet of thick ice. This was the signal for Conrad to get out his skates and to push Gertrude in his sledge right out as far as the island – and sometimes even beyond it. Afterwards they would sit in the warm inglenook by the fisherman's kitchen fire, and Conrad's grandmother would tell them the loveliest stories, while out on the lake the severe cold burst the ice with a thunderous roar, so that great cracks appeared in its surface.

Grandmother's face was made up of a lot of little folds and wrinkles; but her eyes were still bright and clear, and when she told stories, she would look steadfastly ahead of her as though she could see all that she was describing in the darkness at the back of the room. She knew all the local legends, and so many fairy-stories that she could have told a different one for every day of winter.

One evening, when once again the frozen lake was rumbling violently and the echoing thunder of bursting ice went on and on, she said: "Down at the bottom of the lake where the water is deepest lives the Water Monster in a castle of coral, shells and amber, more beautiful than it is possible to describe. All around it lies his garden: the steps are sprinkled with pearls, the beds surrounded by mother-of-pearl shells, and gorgeous jewel-like flowers with gold and silver leaves grow there. Your father, Conrad, once saw the whole splendour of it on a night of full-moon, shining and glittering under the water: but he could never find the place again.

"In the Water Monster's castle there are many beautiful rooms, but one of them contains nothing but a number of shelves on the walls upon which stand a lot of sealed glass bottles with bulging sides. They are full of water, and occasionally they emit a splashing noise, yet there is nothing to be seen in them. The bottles contain the souls of people who have been drowned in the lake. He himself has no soul, but he likes to possess other people's, and hold them captive.

"Listen how the ice out there thunders and echoes when the great cracks appear in it. The Water Monster does that. He does not care to sit at the bottom of the lake as though in a prison of glass, so he pushes against the ice from below with all his strength, so that it cracks with a loud report. But he cannot remove it altogether; for this he, too, must await the wind from the south that brings the thaw.

"If you ever find, in a hidden place, a circular hole in the ice about the size of a waggon-wheel, then keep away from it, for it is the Water Monster's look-out. The edges of the ice at such places are rounded as though polished, and the water never freezes there, even in the bitterest cold. He will sometimes pop his head up to study the weather and see if the south wind is on its way. He likes, too, to skulk beneath the ice and to grab anyone who gets too close to the hole. So beware!"

"Can't the poor souls be saved?" asked Gertrude suddenly.

"Whosoever finds the Flower of Life and wears it on his heart cannot be harmed by the Water Monster as long as its scent endures, and as long as he can resist the temptation of accepting either food or drink at the Water Monster's hands. He may jump into the water, too, knowing that he will be able to move and live in it as though he were on dry land. But the Flower of Life is hard to find. It grows out of the snow in lonely places in the depths of winter, and if it is not plucked within the hour, it dissolves into nothing but perfume. A man from the village is supposed to have seen one many years ago, growing on the island where the pagan shrine is; it was pushing up out of the snow in the centre of the great circle of stones. But he took fright, and ran away."

So grandmama said.

The next day the cold had grown less severe, and it was a beautiful winter's day. After dinner, Gertrude climbed into the sledge, and Conrad pushed her out on to the lake. They planned to go further than usual today: and to circumnavigate the entire island, something they had never done before. After fifteen minutes of non-stop skating, they were near the island, and Conrad stopped to take breath. Then he pushed off again, veering sideways so as to describe a wide arc around the island. Here the ice was still smooth and unmarked and black like polished ebony. When Conrad stopped the sledge, there was nothing to be heard but the whispering of the wind in the dry sedge at the edge of the lake, and the echoing and ringing in the surface of the ice, which was carried from place to place. They could no longer see the village because the island was in the way; it was very lonely on the sunlit surface of the ice.

"I'm frightened," said Gertrude.

"The ice is safe," Conrad answered. "Father said so."

"I am afraid of the Water Monster!" said Gertrude, shuddering.

"There isn't any Water Monster!" cried Conrad. "That's only a fairy-story!"

Suddenly both children gave a start, for with a loud report, a crack appeared in the ice just in front of them, and continued to lengthen and spread away across the lake with a noise like firing pistols and echoing thunder.

"That was him, that was him, I know it was!" whispered Gertrude. "Let us turn back."

But Conrad soothed and comforted her and explained to her that they were exactly half-way, and would reach home just as quickly by going on. So they started off again. Soon they came to a place where a little creek thickly edged with reeds lay in the shelter of the island, a very secluded and remote spot. As Gertrude peered into it, she suddenly cried out:

"I see the Water Monster's look-out! Hurry past it!"

But Conrad, full of curiosity, stopped the sledge and said:

"It isn't dangerous as long as one doesn't go too close. Look, it's just as grandmama described it."

A little way off there was a round hole in the ice; it had smooth edges, and the water within it was slightly ruffled by a light breeze that rustled the encircling reeds and made them whisper.

As the children stood staring at the hole, filled with fear of the sinister thing that might lurk below, the shining golden back of a great fish suddenly appeared, thrashing back and forth in the hole. Then it leapt out and lay floundering on the ice, trying vainly to get back into the water. The children had never seen such a wonderful creature. It had stripes of gold and azure blue, and sparkled in the sunlight.

Conrad couldn't control the fisherman within him.

"I must have him!" he cried, and despite Gertrude's tears and pleading, he ran towards the wriggling fish and put both hands round its slippery body. But hardly had he touched it than the fish sprang with irresistible strength back through the hole in the ice and disappeared in a moment, taking Conrad with it.

Gertrude screamed and cried, but she was helpless to do anything but abandon the sledge and run home as quickly as possible to sob out the dreadful story. A few brave men set out with Conrad's father, and, armed with long poles, they searched all that part of the island that was near the place where Conrad had disappeared. But they found not a trace of him.

Sadness and fear spread through the village at the untimely death of little Conrad; but Gertrude was saddest of all. She cried day and night until she had no tears left. Then a stillness came over her and she resolved to devote her life to rescuing Conrad from his imprisonment. She took a gold locket, a keepsake of her dead mother, and hung it round her neck so that it rested directly over her heart beneath her dress. Then she filled her pockets with bread, and at dawn one Sunday she set out to find the Flower of Life. She thought that it must surely be growing somewhere on the island.

During the night, snow had fallen, and the white, unbroken surface of the lake lay before her, while the island rose up in the dim light like a grey mound of mist. Commending her soul to God, she trudged towards it through the soft snow.

When she reached it, the sun had risen, and Gertrude turned round to look back once more at the village. It lay in the blue winter mist and the smoke from the chimneys on its snow-laden roof-tops rose into the sky against a dark background of forest trees. Then she heard the ringing of the matin bell from the church tower. The gentle sound seemed to wrap itself round her heart as though to pull her towards it. But she turned away and went bravely forward into the deep snow of the island thicket. She kept her eyes down all the time, and took no notice when twigs scratched her and emptied snow down her neck; she forced herself through the densest scrub, and crawled through every possible gap, but all in vain. By now, the minute bell was sounding in the village church and she had searched almost the whole island and still found nothing. She climbed up the hill to the place where the old oaks stretched their gnarled branches into the sky; the flower had grown there once; perhaps it might do so again.

When she got to the top, she saw a lot of tiny footprints in the otherwise unmarked, freshly fallen snow; they all led towards the great ring of stones. She followed them, and found that they passed through a gap in the ring, and on towards two huge megaliths whose summits leaned together, so forming what looked like the entrance to a cave. Out of this wafted warm, springlike air, heavy with the scent of green woodland plants and of violets, so that the snow on the edges of the two stones melted and dripped to the ground.

Gertrude went bravely in and walked down a narrow, dark passage, just the right height for her to be able to do so without stooping. By degrees it became lighter, and the scent of flowers stronger, and at length she entered a hollow space lit by a gentle radiance. The light came from a beautiful naked child with shining white limbs, that lay asleep in the middle of the cave on a bed of violets. The entire walls and ceiling of this room were covered in a profusion of every kind of spring flower, and the thousands of starry flower-heads were turned towards the sleeping child like so many watching eyes.

Gertrude folded her hands and stood silent, unable to take her eyes from the lovely vision, when suddenly a small voice asked: "Who are you, that you enter here before the hour has come?"

Gertrude saw a little man, all in green with an iron-grey beard and a red cap, standing before her and looking at her with friendly eyes. She answered:

"I am seeking the Flower of Life."

The little man replied: "Only an innocent heart and a firm will could have found the way in here. Your wish shall be fulfilled."

Meanwhile many more little men, all dressed like the first, had appeared from the back of the cave, and were staring curiously at Gertrude. But she still could not look away from the lovely child, and when the oldest mannikin saw this, he said:

"You would like to know who the sleeping child is, wouldn't you? It is the Year Child, dear girl, and we are guarding it carefully until its time is ripe. I will tell you how it comes into being. Of all the roses, the last rose of summer is the only one that carries a seed as big as a walnut-shell. We take this seed, and tend it carefully. At the time of the winter solstice, the shell bursts open, and a tiny child lies within. We feed and suckle it with honey from the flowers, and with morning dew, so that it grows, in its sleep, into a great, strong youth, and awakens ready to step out into the wintry world. Flowers and grasses spring up where his feet have trod, and trees break into green leaf in the sunlight of his glances, and a cloud of singing larks flies round his head. It is the future spring who lies sleeping here. Now tell us your own story."

Gertrude did so, and the little men listened in sympathetic silence. Then the oldest mannikin spoke: "Brave girl! You deserve the Flower of Life." So saying, he took a pair of silver scissors from his belt and cut a lock of the Year Child's fine, golden hair and handed it to Gertrude. "Take this hair," he said, "and lay it outside on the snow, and the Flower of Life will spring up."

Then all the little men gave Gertrude their hands, and she went back through the narrow passageway. But it was no longer dark, for the hair she was holding cast a gentle light before her. When she got outside, she knelt down and put the hair on the ground. As though it were aglow, it sank into the hissing snow, which melted away at once, revealing the black earth beneath. A shoot appeared at the spot where the hair had been, and opened out into a shining, blue-green circle of leaves, out of whose centre grew a stalk bearing a single bud. This swelled and reddened: the air was filled with a ringing like the distant singing of larks, and suddenly a glowing red flower opened, streaked with shining threads like the rays of the sun. At the same time such a strong and intoxicating scent filled the air that Gertrude was almost stupefied by it. But she lost no time. With trembling fingers and full of silent worship she plucked the flower, and concealed it in the gold locket over her heart. Then she hurried down the hill to the little cove, where she soon saw the round hole, darkly visible in the white, snow-covered ice. She went towards it, said a short prayer, and – putting her hand on her heart where the precious treasure lay – she jumped bravely into the water. It closed over her; for a little while, it moved and bubbled, and then it lay smooth and shining again, as though nothing had happened. All around was silence and solitude. Only a tiny goldcrest sat on the top of an oak in the sunshine and sang his happy little song, heedless of the snow and ice and cold of winter.

When Gertrude reached the bottom of the lake, she scarcely felt that she was moving in water: but rather, that she was enveloped in some strange element, heavier and colder than air. She saw a winding path of white sand before her, leading gradually downwards, and she began to hurry down it. Feathery water-plants grew on the lake-bottom, and their delicate leaves moved gently whenever a fish swam by. She could make all this out only after her eyes, fresh from the brilliant sunlight, had grown accustomed to the twilit gloom which prevailed beneath the snow-laden ice that covered the lake. Sometimes a whole school of tiny fish swam quickly past her, or stared after her as she walked. Once she was frightened by an enormous pike which was skulking among the water-weeds and goggled at her unpleasantly; huge eels wriggled across her path like snakes, and crabs scuttled away to hide in the rocks as she passed. At last she came to a place that looked like a big, green meadow, and on it someone was standing. As she drew near, she saw with joy that it was Conrad. He had a switch in his hand and was guarding a herd of very ancient, moss-covered carp which were as fat as pigs. She ran quickly towards him, seized his hand, and cried:

"Conrad, come with me! I will save you – I have the Flower of Life!"

The boy pulled his hand away, looked at her strangely, and said:

"Your hand is so warm. I do not know you."

At this, she suddenly realised that he felt as cold as ice; his eyes were empty when he looked at her, and she knew that it was because he had no soul. The little girl began to cry, and one of her tears fell on Conrad's hand. At this, a warm light shone for an instant in his eyes, and it seemed as though he might recognise her. But the next moment, it was gone, and he looked as dull as before.

"I mustn't leave here," he said. "I must herd the carp. If I lose any, the Water Monster will bite me. He has such sharp green teeth."

Sadly Gertrude walked on until she came to the beginning of the Water Monster's garden. The strangest plants grew in it with gold and silver leaves that looked like fish-scales. Others had big red or blue translucent leaves which waved and twisted about as though they were alive. Oddly-shaped fish swam among them; some were transparent like glass, others shone as colourfully as jewels. Then the Water Monster's castle rose before her in the gloaming, and as she approached its gateway, two giant pike – which were mounting guard – suddenly rushed at her gnashing their sharp teeth. But when they felt the effect of the Flower of Life, they beat a hasty retreat, and goggled harmlessly from a distance. So Gertrude entered the castle and stepped into the great hall lined with shells; its floor was composed of a mosaic of fish and precious stones. The Water Monster was sitting alone at a table eating delicious-looking food and washing it down with blood-red wine. He stared at her with cunning eyes, ground his sharp green teeth, and shouted:

"What do you want with me, Earthworm?"

"You must give Conrad back to me," said Gertrude fearlessly.

The Water Monster gave an ugly laugh. "He has to herd my carp: I can't do without him," he said. "Besides, he has such a nice, innocent little soul which pleases me. You have somehow got hold of the Flower of Life; – now see where it will get you!" And he laughed mockingly. But suddenly his expression changed, and with a friendly leer, he said:

"But now that you are my guest, child, come and eat something." With that, he pushed some of the most delicious dishes towards Gertrude, and filled a golden cup with wine. Although she was hungry – for she had eaten nothing all day – and the Water Monster's food smelled very tempting, Gertrude had not forgotten her grandmother's warning. So she declined the invitation, pulled a bit of bread out of her pocket, and ate that instead.

The Water Monster glared at her angrily. "We have a knowing little devil here," he muttered under his breath. Then he thought: "But maybe she doesn't know as much as she thinks she does! I'll keep her hanging about until the scent of the flower has vanished. In three days' time, she'll be herding my carp on the meadow as well!"

Now he pretended to be very friendly, and took Gertrude all over the castle, showing her his treasures – except for the room with the bottles in it. Although she kept her eyes open, she could see no trace of it. So night fell without her having seen Conrad again, for the poor little carp-herd slept with his fish.

On the following morning, the Water Monster had gone, for there had been a thaw in the night, and the river was about to flood its banks, and he couldn't bear to miss a good flood.

All that day Gertrude searched for the hidden room, but she could not find it. In the evening she drew out the gold locket with the flower in it, and found that its scent had already grown much fainter. If she had known that it would lose its power altogether at sunset next day, her fear would have been great. In the morning, she started her search all over again. She thought that she must have opened every door in the castle at least ten times, and she had examined all the walls minutely, but she could not find the secret room. Just as she was about to step out from behind a curtain, she suddenly saw the Water Monster scurrying along the passage. He was carrying a bottle in his hand, and looked furtively around. Then he walked up to a wall and pressed a small golden fish that formed part of its decoration, whereupon the wall slowly opened. The Water Monster disappeared, and came back in a moment without the bottle. Then he went down the passage into the Hall of Shells.

Gertrude stood behind the curtain with a pounding heart, and after a little while, she crept after the Water Monster, and looked through the door of the hall. She saw him empty a huge goblet of wine down his throat, after which he lay down on a mattress and went to sleep. When she could hear his loud snores, she hurried back and pressed the golden fish. The wall swung open, and she stepped into a small, dark room whose windows were strongly barred. But there were so many bottles in it, and her heart sank. For how could she ever hope to find the one that contained Conrad's soul? As she was looking helplessly along the rows of bottles, her eye fell on a little cupboard that she hadn't noticed before. But it was locked. She took out the locket with the Flower of Life, and held it to the keyhole. Immediately, the door sprang open, and she could see that there were only two bottles inside: one full and one empty. She lifted the full one out, and as she looked at it, she clearly heard a splashing sound from within, and she seemed to see Conrad's blue eyes reflected from the glass. So she took the bottle under her arm, and, before leaving the room, she removed the stoppers from all the remaining bottles. The freed souls escaped from them with a soft, singing noise like the humming of bees.

Then Gertrude hurried away, stuffing her pockets with pearls and precious stones as she passed, and ran off to look for Conrad. At last she came across his herd of carp, and after searching for a time, she found him lying in a little hollow fast asleep. She divided the now very faintly scented flower in two halves, and put one in Conrad's jacket pocket: the other she kept herself. Then she held the bottle close to his mouth and carefully took the stopper out. His face suddenly became suffused with colour, warm life flowed through his limbs, and he opened his eyes in astonishment, not knowing where he was. But Gertrude left him no time to remember; she took his hand and pulled him after her. She found the path that had brought her there, and after a while, they found themselves directly beneath the Water Monster's hole, which could be seen silhouetted against the brighter light above. But how could they ever get up to it, weighted down as they were with all the pearls and jewels that Gertrude had divided between them? They were about to abandon the treasure, and Conrad, who could swim, was going to pull Gertrude up to the surface, when suddenly they heard steps on the ice above, and saw dark shadows moving hither and thither. It was the fisherman and his neighbour, the peasant, who were about to make one more effort to get the bodies of their drowned children out from beneath the ice. Soon a long pole with a hook on the end was pushed through the hole and moved haltingly along the lake-bottom. The two children grabbed it unhesitatingly.

When they felt the weight upon the pole, the men

pulled it up, and great was their joy and astonishment when they saw their lost children emerging from the water safe and sound. They had hardly gone a little distance from the hole when there was a rushing and a roaring noise beneath the ice, and the Water Monster popped up out of the hole, shaking his hairy arms and gnashing his teeth. But although he howled and threatened, it was all to no avail.

So the two fathers went happily home with their children, and soon the whole village was joyfully celebrating their miraculous deliverance.

The fathers moved to another district and bought two big farms with the treasures Gertrude had taken from the Water Monster, and Conrad and Gertrude's descendants still live and flourish there to this day.

The Dwarf Wood

One

ON THE EDGE of a wide, green valley through which a clear, swift stream ran lay a large wood. Here the stream could be traced to its source at a spot where many springs flowed together and bubbled out of the mossy ground. It was a lovely place; the birds liked living there and sang merrily through the spring and summer, and people walking among the trees could enjoy the many babbling rivulets as they ran here and there as though in play, appearing unexpectedly between ferns and luxuriant vegetation. The wood was so fresh and green in summertime, and probably it was this coolness that appealed so much to the small tribe of dwarfs which had settled here. They lived at the highest point of the forest-land, where the openings to their caves could be seen behind moss-covered rocks or among the gnarled roots of the big oak-trees.

A wood-cutter had once told of how he had entered the wood late at night and seen a light shining through a cleft in an ancient oak. Curiosity had driven him to approach the tree and to peer through the crack. He saw that the oak was completely hollow, and a lot of dwarfs with pointed green hats and grey coats were sitting at a round table. They were smoking tiny clay pipes and drinking brown stout out of miniature tankards. He was just about to ask them to leave a mugful for him when a voice cried out: "Someone is looking!" and in a moment the whole scene was plunged in darkness. But after that, the wood never seemed the same to him again; it was as though little creatures – kittens or puppies perhaps, for he could not see them – kept running between his legs; he could hear them whimpering as small children do, and all he could think of was to get home as fast as possible.

But on the whole, the little dwarfs were well-disposed towards human beings: if they were left in peace, they did no one any harm. In fact, many tales were told about the good deeds they had done and the many kindnesses they had shown to people. The rumours spread by malicious gossips that they had webbed feet which they were constantly trying to hide were certainly quite untrue. For, in winter, when there was a light covering of snow on the ground, their footprints could be clearly seen to resemble those of very small, beautifully shaped, children's feet. But when the snow lay deep upon the ground, they did not come out, but sat in the depths of their warm caves, living off the supplies of food they had gathered in during the warm months, and busily making many beautiful things out of gold and silver and precious stones.

Outside the wood, they were never visible in their own guise, for they could practise all kinds of magic and had mastered the art of changing themselves into animals. Some people said they had seen them masquerading as hamsters so as to lay in a store of grain for their winter needs; others that they had been seen rifling the nut-trees in the form of squirrels. But no one resented these intrusions, for it was generally recognised that there was truth in the legend that those fields and gardens which were plundered by the dwarfs always produced more and better fruit than the others.

But, as time went on, the lovely green wood with its

many clear streams underwent a great change, for the lower-lying part of it gradually turned into a swamp. For some inexplicable reason, the ground around a dangerous quagmire in that part of the wood began to move, so that it dammed up many of the streams until they overflowed and turned the surrounding land into a great stretch of sluggish fen-water. Poisonous-looking weeds grew thickly round this bog, and its surface was partly covered with a thick, grass-like plant which made it look like solid ground; but to walk upon it was to sink into the slimy morass below, and many an unwary traveller was saved only with difficulty by his companions. The trees became diseased and died, or were blown into the marsh to lie there half submerged with their bare, bleached branches pointing skywards. In the drier places, poisonous snakes increased and multiplied, and so did countless mosquitoes which swarmed so thickly at certain times of the day that no one could venture there for fear of being stung all over. Finally no one dared go into the wood at all, for so many people had simply disappeared in it without a trace, even those who knew it well, and were never heard from again. Besides, there were tales that horrible creatures, something like human beings but with black, shiny skin like snails, lived in the bog. They had cunning little red eyes, and snakelike arms that they could lengthen or retract at will. On their fingers they had suckers with which they could hold on as leeches do, and they spent their time either rolling in the soft, slimy mud with disgusting croaking noises or else hiding in the weeds with only their red eyes peering out. These were on the ends of long stalks, like a snail's, and with them they kept watch for unsuspecting humans or animals that they could seize and drag down to a muddy grave.

No one knew how the little dwarfs had reacted to this unpleasant change in their once cheerful surroundings.

They could hardly be very pleased about it, because the only bit of the wood which had escaped was the small area which lay at a higher level than the rest, and contained all their caves and tree-dwellings. This had become the only part into which it was safe to venture, and a broom-maker who had gone there to collect twigs for his besoms saw one of the little men sitting on a stone. His hat, which was not green but purple with a tiny gold crown round it, lay beside him, and the little fellow sat with his head in his hands as though in deep thought. When the broom-maker made a slight sound, he looked up, and instead of the jolly, pink face most dwarfs have, this one was pale and sad, and when the man asked him what was wrong, he sighed and shook his head as if to say: "There is nothing you can do to help." Then he picked up his hat, slid down from the stone, and vanished into the bushes. Another man had once heard the saddest singing and many little voices raised in what sounded like complaint emanating from the roots of a very old oak in which there was an entrance to one of the dwarf-caves; and a third, a peasant who had taken shelter from a sudden downpour beneath the same tree, said that he had seen the little people carrying water out of their cave in small, shiny pails and emptying it outside with expressions of grave concern on their faces.

Two

Now there lived, in a village whose fields bordered this wood, a poor musician who had an only son named Jonathan. This boy was a Sunday child, and a very special one at that, for he had been born on February 29th – a Leap Year – at exactly twelve noon, and to the sound of church-bells ringing. Such children are said to have a special destiny, and to possess unusual gifts. But there did not seem to be anything unusual about Jonathan. True, he was very nice-looking with lovely golden hair, but he did not appear to possess any special talents, and the other village boys were inclined to tease him for being a dreamer. His father was away a lot, sometimes for several days, for he had to travel from village to village to play at the local dances; so Jonathan wandered about by himself, usually deep in thought. He could lie for hours beside the stream watching the sparkling water, or gazing up at the clouds for ever changing their shape against a background of blue.

His favourite haunt was an old willow-tree which stood at the head of the valley right by the stream. Over the years, the water had washed the earth away from its roots, and it had leaned over more and more, until now its big, round head with a few remaining twigs hung right over the middle of the water. But what it lacked in greenery of its own was replaced by the rich collection of plants that grew inside its hollow stem and covered its large head. For Jonathan, it was like sitting in an orchard, for he could pick raspberries, redcurrants and blackberries from it in season, and many climbing flowers adorned its ancient, rotting trunk in summertime.

One morning, he was sitting on top of the tree among the twigs, looking over at the wood, which had always held a strange fascination for him. As he looked, he noticed a lot of unusual movement and agitation for which he could not account. On the edge of the wood, beneath the bushes, things invisible were scurrying about, and he couldn't exactly make out whether dwarfs or small animals were causing the commotion. No sooner had he begun to realise that something was going on in the wood than he noticed that the meadow, too, was strangely disturbed. Little creatures – he could not decide what they were – flitted between the wild flowers in the long grass, peeking out from time to time and then disappearing, and he could see from the movement of the grass-stalks that they were making for the willow-tree. He had not had time to decide what to do before he felt the old tree shake and tremble, and a sound came from its roots as if they were being gnawed by many sharp little teeth.

Suddenly the tree keeled gently over, and as it came to rest upon the water, Jonathan could see a lot of little hamsters biting through the remaining roots before scrambling on to the willow, which was beginning to float slowly upstream. Now Jonathan could see that several otters had gripped the twigs in their jaws and were towing the tree after them. The stream was narrow, and it would have been quite possible to jump on to the bank, but when the boy tried to get to his feet, he found that something was holding him back. A number of weasels, which had been hiding inside the hollow trunk, had come out, and had him fast by his clothing with their sharp teeth. At the same moment, a long line of squirrels emerged from the meadow and, one after another, they leapt aboard the floating willow. One of them was as white as snow, and it sat on its haunches in front of Jonathan, held up its paws to him as though in supplication, and looked at him so expressively that he knew that it was asking him to stay where he was. He was less afraid when he saw the beautiful, friendly little animal, and waited to see what would happen next.

Scarcely had this odd vessel reached the ill-famed wood than the otters pulled it ashore, and all the animals made for the bank where they were immediately transformed into dwarfs. They wore grey coats and pointed green hats; only the one who had appeared as the white squirrel had a purple hat on which sat a golden crown. This dwarf now addressed Jonathan as follows: "We used this method to get you into the wood because, outside it, we can only appear in animal guise, and, as such, are unable to speak. But we have to ask you to do something for us that only a Sunday child such as yourself can achieve; for you have the power to free us from our great distress. But you must do it of your own free will, and without promise of reward. If you feel that you would like to help us, then we beg you to follow us."

All the little dwarfs made such pathetic faces and held up their hands so beseechingly that Jonathan could not resist them, and climbed from the tree-trunk on to the bank of the stream. His little guides trotted before him, and they went along the top of a narrow dyke which had escaped being flooded, until they reached the higher part of the wood in which the dwarf-dwellings lay as though upon an island. The boy glanced nervously about him as they trod this narrow path, for horrible black water showed here and there in the deceptive, grass-like ground on either side of the dyke, and every now and then the surface stirred and bubbled, and disgusting sounds like smacking lips could be heard. Once, when one of the little dwarfs stumbled and fell a little way down the sloping bank towards the bog, a long, shining black arm shot out of the mud and caught him by one foot; luckily he had grabbed hold of a bush with one hand as he fell, and with the other he reached into a pouch on his belt and sprinkled what looked like red salt on the arm, which immediately loosed its hold and disappeared, while loud snorting and wailing noises came from the morass into which it had sunk. At the same moment, the whole of the slimy surface moved and shook; several revolting, flat heads appeared upon the surface, and stared at the dwarfs with greedy, red eyes, croaking the while like giant frogs, and shaking black, dripping fists out of the surrounding mire.

Meanwhile the path had widened, and the little procession had reached the flat top of the hill where the dwarfs lived. Here many great blocks of moss-covered stone lay among the ancient oaks, and when the dwarf with the purple hat knocked on one of these with his staff, it slid to one side like a door, and exposed the dark entrance to an underground cave.

When Jonathan had climbed down a lot of steps, he and the dwarfs reached a low, vaulted chamber, whose walls and roof sparkled and shone in the lamplight, for they were made of crystal and many-coloured precious stones, all beautifully arranged in mosaic pattern. Against the wall opposite the door there was a tiny throne covered in purple velvet and gold brocade, and before it in a semicircle was a row of smaller chairs. Jonathan was told to sit on a pile of cushions exactly opposite the dwarf with the purple hat, who had seated himself upon the throne, and was obviously the Dwarf King.

When they had sat a while in silence, the king began as follows:

"You have just witnessed the terrible danger we are in, dear Jonathan, and seen what revolting, ugly creatures have moved into our beautiful wood. Instead of the happy sound of clear, swift-running water, all we hear now is the bubble and gurgle of the verminous morass; instead of the song of lovely birds, we hear only the croaking of hideous monsters; instead of the sweet fragrance of flowers and herbs our nostrils are filled with unhealthy fumes and the stench of mud and decay. I will tell you how this came about. In that part of the wood that has been known since time immemorial as the Devil's Bog because of the quagmire in its midst, there lived a race of Bog Gnomes. Their king was named Igglebreach, and he had long wanted to extend his repulsive kingdom until it would swallow up our lovely green wood, but he could not do so unless he

could get the golden bracelet away from us, for to possess this treasure is to possess the wood. We knew how much he wanted to get hold of the bracelet, and so we were on our guard. We had hidden it in our treasure-house behind seven iron doors, and believed it to be safe enough. But one day a strange dwarf came to us, saying that he had been sent to exchange precious stones, of which there were but few in the kingdom from which he came. He carried a large bag of valuable pearls, and of these we possessed hardly any; but precious stones we have in plenty. The stranger had a grim and cunning look and his face was an odd, blackish colour; his movements, too, were smooth and snakelike; but we thought these must be the characteristics of his tribe, and trusted him because his pearls were faultless and his way of talking inspired confidence. So, when we had given him a seemly welcome, we took him to our treasure-house, where he seemed amazed at the riches it contained, and could not praise our delicate gold and silver artefacts or our collection of jewels enough. As we did not suspect him, we showed him everything, even the precious bracelet itself, though without, of course, revealing its significance. And he did not seem to pay it much attention; so we began to trade precious stones for pearls, and when we had come to a satisfactory agreement, we left the treasure-house and proceeded to the banqueting-hall, where it was the custom to drink to successful enterprises with our own home-made wine. But, when we got there, the stranger had disappeared. No one had seen him go, and we searched and called for him in vain. Suddenly I felt a sense of foreboding: I returned with my people to the treasure-house and found that my fears were only too well-founded, for the golden bracelet, our most precious possession, had gone. Obviously the stranger had been an emissary from the King of the Bog Gnomes, maybe even the king himself in the shape of a dwarf. We knew that he possessed the Stone of Mutability which could enable him to assume any disguise, although there always remained something of the Bog Gnome in his appearance. That was why he had such a grim and cunning look, such a dark skin, such snakelike movements and, above all, such cold, clammy hands which, when I welcomed him, had made me shudder at their touch.

"The most swift-footed among us set out at once in the direction of the quagmire, but they could not catch the thief: they just caught a glimpse of him as he reached the morass and waved the shining bracelet aloft, shouting in triumph, before jumping down into the black ooze, which swallowed him up."

Three

When the Dwarf King had reached this point in his story, he was quiet for a while, and during the ensuing silence, the other dwarfs sat and gazed into space with melancholy expressions on their faces. Then the king began his tale again:

"From this time onwards, calamity befell our wood. The Bog Gnomes, no longer opposed by the power of magic, gradually dammed up the springs and blocked their outlets, so that what had once been fresh, sweet-smelling woodland turned into a stinking bog, which is the breeding-place of such creatures as you have seen. And they are still adding to their kingdom. Some of our caves are already flooded, and we have had to leave them. Soon the narrow dyke, our only link with the outside world, will be under water too, and we shall be forced to leave our dear homes and migrate to another place. We are powerless against our enemies, except for the red salt which we make from certain secret herbs; this can be used as a weapon in case of attack, for it burns their slimy limbs like fire, and eventually kills them. But many of our brothers who had no time to use the salt, or had forgotten to carry some with them, have been dragged down into the bog, never to be seen again.

"This, then, is the terrible danger which besets us: and this is the reason why we so desperately wanted you to listen to our plea for the help which only you can give. You have the power, as the very special Sunday child that you are, to get back our golden bracelet for us, for evil spells cannot harm you. If you have the courage to seek out the enemy upon his own ground, we will provide you with the ways and means to snatch back from him the treasure which alone can restore our peace and happiness."

Jonathan thought of his experiences on the way to the Dwarf Kingdom, and shuddered. He was deeply afraid of the dreadful creatures that had appeared above the slime. When the Dwarf King saw this, he ran from his throne to kneel at Jonathan's feet, and all the other dwarfs did the same, and as they held up their hands to him in supplication, Jonathan could not resist them, and made up his mind to attempt the perilous task. When the dwarfs realised this, their faces shone with pleasure, and they took him to the banqueting hall where a splendid feast had been prepared. Marvellous dishes the names of which Jonathan had never even heard covered the tables, and were washed down with richly perfumed wine in golden goblets. Through the crystal walls, the kitchen could be seen, where minute chefs in white caps and aprons ran about dishing up one delicious thing after another, and Jonathan was delighted with it all.

He spent that night with the dwarfs, and slept soundly upon silken pillows. Next morning, the king told him the plan he had devised to regain the bracelet, and when he had explained it, he went on to say: "There is only one danger, dear Jonathan, and that is that you may allow your eyes to be deceived by evil sorcery. The cunning Gnome King will realise at once what your purpose is, and he will do everything in his power to prevent you. In order that you may be able to tell truth from trickery, I will give you this eye-glass. Keep it safely, for if you put it to your eye, you will be able to tell at once what is true and what is false."

With that, he hung a round glass set in gold round Jonathan's neck, and said: "Now I will prove the power of the magic glass to you. Look through it at the animal that will appear before you."

The next moment, the dwarf turned into a white squirrel. But when Jonathan looked at it through the glass, he could clearly see the Dwarf King in his purple hat; and as soon as he removed the glass, there stood the little white squirrel again. When the king had reassumed his own shape, he said:

"You know the plan which I have just explained to you; if you follow my directions with courage and determination, it cannot go wrong. The happiness of a harmless and peace-loving people lies in your hands. Now act cleverly and fearlessly, as you have promised to do!"

Four

Next morning Jonathan set out on his adventure, accompanied by a dwarf who was to serve him as guide. Once outside the wood, his companion changed into a weasel and ran ahead of him, showing him the quickest way to the Devil's Bog. This was a bottomless quagmire, in which patches of green slime alternated with areas of black, muddy water; here and there, floating islands of grass were just capable of bearing a very light weight without sinking: but to tread too heavily upon their deceptive surface was to be sucked slowly and irretrievably into the moving black mud below. It was a lonely spot, avoided by everyone because of its evil reputation. On the edge of the bog stood a very old willow-tree, half destroyed by lightning, hollow and only just alive. The entrance to the Gnome King's underground kingdom lay within the hollow trunk of this tree. When they reached it, the weasel ran up Jonathan's leg and turned into a little shrew-mouse so that it could more easily hide in his waistcoat pocket.

Jonathan mastered the feeling of dread which overcame him when the damp, foetid air wafting up from the dark hole filled his nostrils; he commended his soul to God and bravely walked down the many steps that led to a dark, dank passageway. It was dimly lit by the phosphorescence of mouldering wood. At last he reached a door which was guarded by two enormous toads, chained, like watch-dogs, to rings on either side. As soon as they saw him, they puffed themselves up, and gave forth a barking croak. At this, the door opened, and one of the hideous black Bog Gnomes stuck his head round it, but he turned green with fright when he saw Jonathan, and hastily slammed it shut again. A lot of buzzing, murmuring and croaking could be heard at first: then there was silence. Suddenly the door was thrown wide open, and a bright light shone upon a beautifully liveried footman, who bowed deeply as he invited Jonathan to step inside. To his surprise, the toads had turned into dogs with short, bandy legs; they wagged their tails, but had a rather nasty look in their bulging eyes.

Jonathan passed through a glittering ante-room into a circular hall whose magnificence astounded him. The walls were formed out of the stems of countless water-lilies, tall enough for their flat leaves to form the ceiling. They gave forth a greenish-golden light, and between them Jonathan could see many-coloured water-plants among whose leaves shoals of fish swam, gleaming like phosphorescent jewels. It was like looking into a tank of tropical fish swimming in clear, sunlit water.

Hardly had Jonathan taken all this in before the King of the Bog Gnomes appeared, beautifully dressed, handsome and smiling, and yet with a look of cunning in his eyes which ill became his bright image. A dazzling train of retainers followed him in, and took their places on various chairs and thrones round the hall. Finally two courtiers carried in the infant heir to the Bog Kingdom; he lay upon a golden shield and was dressed in purple and gold. The baby had a pretty face, somewhat marred by black shadows round his eyes, which squinted slightly. When he had been placed in a special baby-chair next to his father's throne, the sound of trumpets rang out, and the king spoke:

"I am well aware that you are a messenger from the Dwarf Kingdom: what is your purpose in coming here?"

"I have come," said Jonathan, "to fetch back the golden bracelet that you have obtained from the dwarfs through trickery!"

King Igglebreach smiled in a most friendly manner, and said: "You have allowed yourself to be taken in, my boy, by the talk of the cunning dwarfs. What do I know about any bracelet, and, if I did, of what use would it be to me who possess all the pearls and jewels I need? You are young and inexperienced, and the miserly dwarfs are using you to undertake tasks they themselves are too cowardly to perform. Have they offered you any reward? Of course not; their only interest is to hoard their treasure and never to part with any of it. I will prove to you that King Igglebreach has a more generous nature."

With that, he made a sign, and two pages came in, each carrying a golden dish filled to the brim with the most beautiful pearls and precious stones. "I will make you a present of this treasure," said Igglebreach. "As you probably have no idea of its value, I can tell you that to possess it will make you richer than anyone else in the whole country, and that you will be able to buy a dukedom with it! So take this small gift, and go on your way."

In the meanwhile, the shrew-mouse had crept out of Jonathan's waistcoat pocket and was tugging as hard as it could at the eye-glass that hung round his neck. Jonathan was so confused by the unexpected turn of events that he didn't notice it at first, but at last he realised that the little creature was reminding him to put the glass to his eye. What a terrible change took place in the scene that had so delighted him only a moment before! No sooner was the glass before his eye than he saw, instead of the dazzling company, a disgusting gathering of black, slimy monsters, which stared at him with cunning, red eyes and furious expressions. Instead of golden chains they wore hissing adders round their necks, and their golden chairs had turned into rotting tree-stumps with slugs crawling all over them. The jewels and pearls had become dirty black pebbles or empty snail-shells, and the king's son was a little horror covered in warts. The lovely shining walls of the hall had disappeared, and now Jonathan seemed to be looking into a dark bog filled with leeches, toads, newts and other ugly creatures.

At the same moment, a howling, croaking and screaming filled the air, and the gnomes hurled themselves at him, but an invisible screen protected him and prevented them from touching him. The moment had come to carry out the Dwarf King's plan. Jonathan waited his opportunity, and seized the baby Bog Prince by the scruff of his neck, while he reached into his pocket with the other hand, drew out a pouch full of the red salt the dwarfs had given him, and shouted:

"If you don't hand over the bracelet at once, King Igglebreach, your son has not long to live!"

The king and all the other gnomes turned green with fear, and shrank away from the dreaded salt. The king cried out:

"Stop, and you shall have anything you want!"

He beckoned to the master of his treasure-house, and whispered in his ear. Soon the creature returned with a large, heavily bejewelled bracelet, and was about to hand it to Jonathan. But the shrew-mouse gave him a smart prod, and Jonathan understood the warning signal at once.

"It's the wrong bracelet!" he shouted and held the red salt over the struggling, screaming gnomelet. "Stop!" shrieked Igglebreach, grey-green with rage and fear, for he loved the little monster in his own way. Then he hurried off and returned after a while with a smooth, oval bracelet of massive gold, just large enough to slip over a small hand. When the shrew-mouse saw the bracelet, it began a jubilant squeaking, so that Jonathan knew that this time it was the true one.

And so he regained possession of the treasure, and climbed back up from the Bog Kingdom without further incident.

Five

When Jonathan got back to Dwarf Wood with the precious bracelet, all the dwarf dwellings rang with cries of jubilant delight. The dwarfs danced about, turned somersaults in the green grass, and couldn't contain their joy. At the same time, moans, whines and melancholy croaking emanated from the boggy end of the wood; everywhere there was a movement as of wriggling things rolling and wallowing and as their slimy home retreated and dried up, so these sounds faded away, and the horror disappeared for ever.

"You helped us with no promise of reward," said Purple Hat to Jonathan. "That was how it had to be. But now we may show you our gratitude."

He gave him armfuls of gold and precious stones, and thus laden, Jonathan returned to the village and his home. His father had given him up for lost, and was not a little astonished to see him returning not only unharmed, but able to make a wealthy man of him. He bought a fine farm bordering on Dwarf Wood, and when he died, Jonathan – who had grown up in the meanwhile – acquired the ownership of this wood as well, now green and fresh again, and full of clear-running streams. But the Devil's Bog had turned into dry, black land on which no grass or trees grew, and no living creature was ever seen. And nothing more was heard of the Bog Gnomes. Probably they all dried up with the mud.

The Cairn

OUT IN THE FIELDS among the corn there lay a cairn. It was said to have been a burial place for giants in olden times. A huge oak-tree stood on top of it, and white-thorn and wild rose-bushes grew all around it.

One Saturday afternoon in summer, when I was still such a little boy that the corn reached over my head, I went to the cairn to look for a piece of wood to make a catapult with. When I got there, I sat down on the gnarled roots of the oak tree, and gazed out over the fields. It was a very hot day: sometimes a breath of warm air stirred the ripe corn so that the ears whispered among themselves. The blue sky was full of great, white, fluffy clouds, and insects buzzed and hummed all around me as I watched the butterflies playing their summer games among the corn-stalks.

I had been sitting like that for quite a little while, too lazy to move, when I heard a sound in the bushes nearby, a rustling in the grass and small twigs snapping. At first I paid no attention to it, for a lot of field-mice had nests in the mound. But then I heard a little voice saying: "Hacka-block, bring out the big crown as well!"

At this, I got a fright, for there was no one to be seen. But low down among the bushes, where there was a small open space, I saw something shining. Leaning forward, I peered cautiously through the twigs, and saw two little men with long grey beards and dressed all in grey, laying out a quantity of gold plate and shining jewels in the sun. A third, whose white beard almost touched the ground and who wore a fine gold circlet on his head, was standing watching them. Then more little dwarfs came out of a small cave-mouth that was hidden under a bush. Their arms were full of golden goblets, vessels made of gold, and a multitude of precious stones which they placed on the ground beside the rest. Finally the last dwarf emerged lugging a large golden crown studded with sparkling jewels; after which, they all helped to arrange the treasure in tidy rows, where it lay flashing and glittering in the sunlight. As I leaned forward to get a better view, I must have made a noise, for all of a sudden all the little men looked up from their work with furious faces, and one of them shouted:

"He can see us! He must be a Sunday child!"

"Then he must die!" cried another.

Before I had time to think, the dwarfs were swarming all over me, and in a trice my feet were bound so tightly with fine chains of gold that I could not move an inch.

"What do you want of me?" I cried. "I have done you no harm!"

"You will betray us!" said the dwarf with the golden circlet round his head, who was their king. "You will tell those greedy human beings in the village, and they will come with their picks and shovels and dig up the mound under which we have lived for thousands of years."

"We will stab him to death!" screamed one dwarf.

"He shall eat poisonous toadstools!" yelled another.

Now I was really frightened, for the little men were making most ferocious faces and some of them had gone back into the cave and returned with sharp little swords which they brandished at me.

"I will never betray you, you little dwarfs!" I shouted. "Let me go, and you shall never have cause to regret it!"

The Dwarf King stroked his white beard thoughtfully: then he beckoned to the other dwarfs, and they all gathered round in a circle and had a whispered consultation. Now and then, one of them would turn and glance in my direction. At last the king held up three fingers and said something, at which they all nodded their heads. Then they separated again. The king came up to me and said:

"You did not mean to spy on us and we have only ourselves to blame if you saw some of our secrets, for we ought to have made certain beforehand that you were not a Sunday child. And Cracklesnap says that he has often observed you in secret, and that he is of the opinion that you can be trusted. But you must solemnly swear never to speak of what you have seen today, or perhaps may see in the future."

I promised, and when I had done so, the dwarfs untied me, and I was allowed to stay and watch them. The king sat down beside me on a tree-root and said: "Every summer, when the corn is ripe and it is really lonely here, we bring our golden treasure and our jewels out to clean them and let the sun shine on them."

Meanwhile the other dwarfs were busily occupied in rubbing the goblets, plate and jewels with soft cloths, so that they shone even more brightly than before. I asked:

"Have you lived in this mound for a long time?"

"You humans who are renewable every fifty years would probably call it a long time," he replied.

I told him that people thought the mound was a cairn in which giants had once buried their dead.

"People are stupid," he said. "When we first came out of Asia and moved into this mound, the great flood had just passed, and there were no human beings in the world – or giants either."

By this time the dwarfs had finished their work and had begun to carry all the things back into the cave again. The king stood up, lifted his hand and said:

"Remember your promise!"

Before entering the cave, he turned round once more and said: "If you want to, you can come and visit us sometimes on Saturday at about this time. If you ever have a special reason for wanting to speak to us, knock three times on this stone, which marks the opening to our cave, and someone will come out and ask you what you want. But never call us unless you have a good reason!"

I often saw the little dwarfs again, for I could hardly wait for Saturday afternoon to come round so that I could go in search of them. Then I would watch their games, or they would tell me stories. Soon I knew them all by name. There was Hackablock, the strongest one, who could move the stone away from the cave entrance with one hand. Cracklesnap was the liveliest of them, and could climb about in the bushes like a squirrel. Groundsel was the smallest and clumsiest, but he could turn a fine somersault, and Trippitfast danced the dwarf-dance better than any of the others. All of them could make beautiful, delicate things out of gold, ivory and precious stones, and they did very fine wood-carvings, too. Spinnerfine could spin finer gold thread than a spider could, and Shuttlefoot wove lovely materials out of gold and silk. But Murmurmouth and Hummerharp were my two favourites. Murmurmouth could tell thousands of stories. He often used to sit on my knee for hours, stroking his long beard, and telling stories of elves, giants, dragons and hob-goblins. Hummerharp had a beautiful harp he had made out of gold and ivory with siren-hairs for strings. When he played, he sang many old dwarf-songs in a fine, tenor voice, and although I couldn't understand the words – for they were in dwarf-language – I liked listening to him very much. But King Rustlebeard was never there; he always stayed inside the cave, for the open air did not suit him very well.

So autumn came. One evening, I was sitting at home in my warm corner behind the stove and thinking about the stories Murmurmouth had told me. Father was talking to a stranger who was paying us a visit. He was an archaeologist, and used to go searching for old bones, old bits of pottery and implements used long ago by people who had altogether ceased to exist. At first I did not pay much attention to what they were saying, but suddenly I became aware that they were talking about the cairn.

"So I can have your permission to have the old mound thoroughly excavated?" said the stranger.

"I would be grateful if you could spare the old oak-tree that stands on top of it," said my father: "but of course you may fell it if it gets in the way of your research."

I got a dreadful shock and, without thinking what I was doing, I jumped out from behind the stove and shouted:

"But it isn't a cairn at all, father; the mound was there before there were any human beings – or giants either!"

"What do you know about it, boy?" said my father, and the archaeologist looked at me through his spectacles, and laughed. I begged my father not to allow the cairn to be interfered with, but I could not tell him why, so he ended by getting cross and sending me out of the room. I ran straight through the garden and across the fields. It was a clear autumn night, and the moon lit the way for me.

When I got to the mound, I knocked three times on the stone. After a little while, Hackablock came out of the cave with a little lantern in his hand and asked me what I wanted. I told him everything I had heard, and he was so upset that he dropped the lantern, which went out. Then

he ran quickly back into the cave-opening, and in a few moments cries of dismay could be heard within the mound and soon afterwards King Rustlebeard himself appeared, and all the other dwarfs behind him. Now I had to tell my story all over again, while they stood around me with sorrowful faces.

"I thought this would happen one day," said King Rustlebeard. "Let us move out this very night and seek refuge with King Hardground deep in the Harz Mountains. He will be sure to welcome us."

The dwarfs all went sadly back into the mound and came out after a while loaded with sacks containing their treasures. They each held out a little hand to me and said their goodbyes. Some sobbed aloud, and cried: "O, our dear home-mound where we have lived for so many thousand years!" Then they lit their torches and started on their journey. Rustlebeard led the way with his white ivory staff in his hand, then came Hackablock, Murmurmouth, Hummerharp, Cracklesnap – all heavily laden with their sacks – and all the other dwarfs. Groundsel brought up the rear; and so they disappeared into the night. For a little while I could still hear their lamentations and see the little procession winding its way across the stubble fields: here and there a torch flickered: then there was silence, and the last I saw of my little friends was what looked like an illuminated caterpillar toiling up the foothills of the distant mountains.

Next day, the archaeologist went up to the cairn with a lot of workmen and supervised them while they dug up the whole mound. But they found nothing except an empty beer-bottle which some harvest-hand had left behind.

But the little dwarfs had gone, and never came back.

The Christmas Country

1 *Werner and Anna*

IN THE LAST house in the village, just where the forest begins, there lived a poor widow with her two children, Werner and Anna. The few vegetables she grew in her small garden, the milk which her one goat provided and the few shillings she earned at her spinning-wheel were barely enough to support the little family, and so the children, too, had to do their bit. And they did so gladly, for the only way they could earn a little money was by going into the beautiful forest and thoroughly exploring it in a search for things to sell in the town. In springtime, they would gather big bunches of golden cowslips and blue anemones and, later, sweet-scented lilies-of-the-valley where they poked their heads up among the fallen beech-leaves. The woodruff grew there, with its flowering sprays like tiny individual trees, which must be picked before the white flower-buds opened if they were not to fade and lose their strong, spicy scent. But once they had dried out, pretty wreaths could be woven from them out of which a sweet aroma still arose; or they could be tied into little bunches for the townspeople of quality to season their wine with, giving it the dew-fresh fragrance of early spring.

Later in the year, the bright crimson of wild strawberries shone near the ground, half hidden by their creeping foliage, and while the children of wealthier parents ran into the forest to feast on these, or maybe pick one here and there to take home to their mothers, Werner and Anna would sit on the forest floor picking them busily: "the good ones for keeping, the bad ones for eating". But they did this happily, vying with one another as to who could pick the most, and singing as they worked.

After the strawberries came the red whortleberries which ripened in the moss under the pine-trees, and looked like a forest of dwarf plum-trees as they stood close together beneath the big pines covered in their tiny, plum-coloured berries. These, too, the children gathered, and their fingers were stained a deep blue as they filled their baskets. Then it was off to the heath where the bilberries grew. Their delicate flowers look like tiny, pink-edged porcelain bells, and their coral-like fruit tastes delicious when it is made into preserve and eaten with apple sauce.

The children learned a lot about what the townspeople liked and would pay a few coppers for from old Lizzie, who drove to town every day with her ancient horse and creaking cart filled with vegetables, and would take whatever the children had collected and sell it for them. So they looked for pretty as well as useful things in the great forest: delicate mosses and reddish lichens branched like coral, and resembling tiny pine-trees. Or others from which minute, trumpet-like flowers grew; there were many different kinds, and all were popular with the townspeople. For they kept their bright colours for a long time and could be arranged in a dish to make a little garden which lasted through the dark winter months and brought the beauty of the forest into the dark houses of the town.

When autumn came, and the stormy winds brought dead branches down from the trees, the children would gather bundles of wood and pile them under the overhanging roof of the house. As they collected the wood and carried the bundles home, they looked forward to the long winter evenings when the fire crackled merrily on the hearth, casting bright reflections on walls and ceilings, while apples fizzled as they baked in the oven, and their mother told fairy-stories as she worked at her whirring spinning-wheel. And so Christmas drew near, and the very mention of the word made the children's eyes shine with excitement. And yet there was little enough to show for the day when it came. There might be a tiny Christmas tree with a few candles, apples and nuts and a couple of gingerbread men hanging on it; under it a warm winter woolly for each of them and, if they were lucky, a simple, cheap toy or a new slate; that was all. And yet a special light seemed to shine out of the little candles and the golden star on the tip of the tree, which illuminated the whole year, and lit up the children's eyes whenever the word "Christmas" was mentioned.

One winter's night, when they were sitting cosily by the fire and their mother had just finished telling a Christmas fairy-tale, Werner suddenly asked: "Mother, where does Father Christmas live?"

His mother let the thread run through her fingers to the merry whirring of the spinning-wheel, and answered:

"Father Christmas? He lives behind the forest in the mountains. But nobody knows the way to his country; whoever tries to find it discovers that he is going round in circles, and the birds hop from twig to twig and laugh at him. Father Christmas has gardens in the mountains, and halls and underground caverns, and his helpers work busily in them day and night, making Christmas presents. Silver and gold apples and nuts grow in the gardens, and fruit made of marzipan hangs on the trees, and the great halls are stacked high with thousands of the most beautiful toys in the world. There are rooms full of dolls dressed in muslin, wool, velvet and silk . . ." "Ah," said little

Anna with shining eyes. " . . . and other rooms filled with drums and swords and guns, cannons and lead soldiers."
"Oh!" cried Werner, and his eyes sparkled.

He kept thinking of this story, and of how marvellous it would be if he could succeed in finding his way to this wonderland. Once he walked as far as the mountains, but, although he searched, he could find nothing but valleys and hills and trees. The streams which flowed there chattered and murmured just like any ordinary stream, but they did not reveal their secret; woodpeckers tapped the trees with their long beaks and flew away just as they did in the forest near home, and there was nothing special about the squirrels as they played their games high in the tree-tops. Werner felt that *someone* must be able to tell him the way to the wonderful Christmas Country. But the people he asked only laughed at him, and when he complained to his mother that no one would tell him the way, she laughed too, and told him not to think about it any more. It was only a fairy-story she had told them that night, she said.

But Werner couldn't stop thinking about it, though he never mentioned it to anyone after that. Except occasionally to his sister when they were out gathering wood, and together they would dream of the wonders of the Christmas Country.

2 *The Little Bird*

One morning shortly before Christmas, Werner took the chopper from the kitchen and went into the forest, for the forest-keeper, who liked him, had once again given him permission to cut down a little fir-tree for Christmas Eve. The children had long ago chosen the one they wanted, and were agreed that it was the prettiest in the whole forest. It grew far off in a clearing under an old beech-tree, and was just the right size and shape.

It was a fine, mild winter's day, the sun shone down out of a cloudless sky, and the forest floor was lightly powdered with snow; just the right sort of day for the little birds of the forest who stay with us all through the winter. The air was full of the cheeping and calling of tits and goldcrests which flew about in the tree-tops searching the boughs for insects. When Werner had reached the old beech-tree with the little fir beneath it, he sat down on a stump to have a rest. It was as quiet as an empty church; the only sound was the gentle gurgle of a stream that flowed darkly between its snow-whitened banks, and in the distance the occasional screech of a jay. Werner began to dream of the Christmas Country again, and he was soon so overcome with the longing to see all the beauty it must contain that he cried out loud: "Oh, if only *someone* could show me the way to the Christmas Country!"

Then a louder sound like tinkling laughter rose from the ripples of the stream, a wood-mouse peeped out of her hole in a tree-trunk and chuckled in a high voice, and the summit of the old beech-tree rocked and rustled as though it were shaking its head at such foolishness. But a sudden fine, clear twitter came from the little fir-tree in front of Werner; it was a blue-tit, hopping from twig to twig, and constantly calling out:

"Ask me! Ask me!"

"What should I ask you?" said Werner. "What do you know?" The little bird rose into the air, turned a neat somersault, landed on the fir-tree again, and twittered:

"I know the way! I know the way!"

"Then show it to me," said Werner quickly.

The little bird began to twitter and chirp again, but

Werner understood what it was saying. "You were good to me," it sang. "You protected my babies, my ten little babies. I know the way, and I'll show it to you. Quick! Quick!" And the bird flew on to the next tree, while Werner began to follow it. He understood, now, the meaning of its song, for he remembered how he had saved a nest of baby blue-tits from a marauding jay early that year. The poor mother had been trying to defend them, but she could never have succeeded if Werner had not chased the huge bird away. So now the little tit was showing him her gratitude. She flew ahead of him, always following the stream, until they reached the mountains. Here the ground began to slope upwards, and they entered a valley that grew ever narrower as they climbed up between steep walls of stone. The stream, meanwhile, had disappeared beneath a smooth-faced cliff whose summit was crowned with giant pine-trees. Suddenly the little bird called from somewhere high up and far away: "Soon! Soon!"

Werner sat down on a rock and looked up at the rock-wall. It was completely smooth, without hand- or foot-holds, and overgrown with moss and lichen. So, as there was no opening visible in its steep surface, Werner sat and waited. The stream flowed noisily into a deep cleft under the rock, and there was no other sound except for the monotonous soughing of the wind in the branches of the pine-trees. At last he heard a little fluttering noise above him, and a hazel-nut fell into his lap.

"Take it – take it!" called the blue-tit. "Bite it open!"

Werner took the nut and examined it. It looked quite like an ordinary nut, except that it rattled when he shook it, as though there were something hard inside it. So he cracked it with his teeth, and there, inside, was a tiny golden key. In the meantime, the little bird had flown to the cliff-face where it hung on with its little claws and pecked and pecked around until pieces of moss and lichen flew about. At last it twittered: "Here – here!"

Werner drew nearer, and saw a little keyhole rimmed with silver. The golden key fitted it exactly, and when Werner turned it in the lock, a strange ringing sound could be heard, and a heavy door opened of itself in the rock-face, so beautifully carved in it as to be quite invisible from the outside. At the same moment, warm, bluish vapour streamed out of the opening, and the air was full of the scent of wax candles after they are blown out, and of smouldering pine-needles.

"O, how that smell reminds me of Christmas!" said little Werner.

But the bird called out: "Inside! Inside! Quick, quick!"

Werner, who was a little afraid, had scarcely entered the dark passage when he felt a draught behind him, and found himself in complete darkness: for the door had silently closed itself behind him. Now his heart sank, for he realised that he could no longer turn back. But he knew that it was no use to stand there trembling, so he forced himself to feel his way along the pitch-dark passageway.

3 *The Christmas Country*

Soon it began to grow lighter, and in a little while, he stepped out into a wonderful region unlike any he had seen before. Although it was warm there, it was not the warmth of summer that lapped him round, but rather the sort of warmth that well-heated rooms have, and it was heavy with all manner of delicious smells. There was no sun in the sky, and yet an even brightness enveloped everything. He could not see very much of the region itself, for the high rock-wall through which he had come towered behind him, while the view ahead was obscured by many tall bushes on which the strangest fruits grew. As he walked between these bushes in ever-increasing astonishment, he came upon a wide avenue which led to a distant building. Large apple-trees grew on either side of it, and they were covered in gold and silver apples. Gnome-like old men with iron-grey beards and a number of young children were busily picking the apples and filling large baskets with them; some were already brimming with the glittering fruit. But no one took any notice of little Werner, who went on walking in silent amazement towards the building, which he could now recognise as a large castle with high towers and gilded domes and roof-tops. On either side of the avenue lay many fields, and these were divided into beds, and planted with various shrubs and plants. Here, too, there was great activity; small, colourfully dressed and gnome-like, the workers hastened to harvest each field and to load what they had gathered into small, two-wheeled carts drawn by tiny, shaggy ponies.

As Werner approached the castle, he noticed a smell of gingerbread, and the nearer he got, the stronger it grew, until he suddenly realised that the castle was built entirely of this delightful sweetmeat. The foundations consisted of great blocks of the stuff, and the walls were made out of smooth ginger biscuits; these were decorated with a mosaic of almonds and candied peel. There were marvellous eaves of raised marzipan beneath the cupolas of the towers; the balustrades, galleries and balconies were delicately wrought in icing sugar, magnificent chocolate statues stood in golden niches, and the windows were made of transparent, many-coloured lozenges and acid-drops; the entire place really looked good enough to eat! The decorative front door had a bell-pull made of barley-sugar and Werner summoned all his courage and gave it a tug. But no bell sounded within: just a very loud: "Cock-a-doodle-do!" which made the little boy jump backwards. Then the cry was repeated once again, fading like an echo into the interior of the building until it died out altogether. At this moment, the door swung open, and a strange personage appeared whom, if it had not lived and breathed, Werner would have taken for a large marionette.

"Great Crumblecake!" said this jolly person. "Visitors? This is an odd state of affairs!" And he showed his surprise and delight by throwing all his limbs right up over his head, which was a somewhat disturbing sight. Then, while his legs and arms waved ceaselessly back and forth, he asked: "What do you want then, my boy?"

"Does Father Christmas live here?" asked little Werner.

"Certainly he does," said the marionette, "and his Honour is at home, but busy, very busy." With that, he bowed to the little boy and beckoned him to follow him, moving forwards and sideways and jerking all the time, because this was the only way he could get about. He took Werner through a vestibule whose walls were of marzipan and whose ceiling rested upon pillars of polished chocolate, to a door which was guarded by two enormous wooden nutcrackers who wore full dress uniform and bearskins on their heads. Here he left Werner, and went in. The nutcrackers stared at Werner with a grin on their wooden faces. Then the marionette came out again, bowed sideways, and said: "His Honour bids you to come in!" At this, the nutcrackers stood to attention, presented arms, and clattered their wooden jaws until the noise resembled a roll of drums.

When Werner entered Father Christmas's room, he was very surprised, because he did not look in the very least like he had imagined him, nor as he appeared in picture-books. True, he did have a very long white beard, but on his head he wore a blue cap embroidered with gold thread, and otherwise he was wearing a long yellow silk dressing-gown as he sat and wrote in a large book. This dressing-gown was covered in such wonderful needle-work patterns that it looked like the illustrations in a book. There were soldiers and dolls, puppets and every kind of Noah's Ark animal, drums, pipes, violins; trumpets, swords and guns, wreaths and tinsel, sun, moon and stars.

Father Christmas put down his pen, and said: "How did you get here, boy?"

Werner answered: "The little bird showed me the way."

"There hasn't been a visitor here for hundreds of years," said Father Christmas. "It is a great achievement for such a little fellow, and you shall have, as your reward, a guided tour of the whole place. I have no time, at the moment, to take you around myself, but my daughter can show you everything. Goldflame, come here!" he called, "we have a visitor!"

A rustling sound came from the next room, and a beautiful little girl appeared, dressed all in spun gold so that she flashed and glittered from head to foot. She wore a crown of gold tinsel on her head on the top of which a live flame burned.

"Oh, this is delightful!" said the little girl, took Werner's hand and cried: "Come with me, little unknown boy!" and together they ran out of the room.

4 *Father Christmas's Store-Houses*

Soon they entered a wide passage down both sides of which stood row upon row of wooden horses on wheels; they were tethered to rings in the walls, and there were greys and bays, sorrels and blacks, even piebald horses.

"Choose one for yourself!" said Goldflame.

Werner picked out a beautiful, highly varnished dapple-grey with great big spots painted on its hindquarters; and Goldflame mounted a shining black horse. "Gee up!" she cried, and immediately the horses rolled off down the passage, so fast that Werner's hair was blown back from his face and the flame on the little girl's crown streamed out behind her head. When they reached the door at the end of the passage, she called out: "Ho, there!" At this, it opened of itself, and they sped through into an enormous hall and drew rein right in its centre. There they dismounted from their horses, and Goldflame said: "This is called the Hall of Lead." The walls were entirely covered with open cupboards whose shelves were stacked high with countless boxes of toys made of lead, from whole armies of lead soldiers to farm animals, winter sports scenes, menageries, anything, in fact, that can be made out of lead. Little black-bearded dwarfs ran nimbly up and down ladders, loading the boxes on to trolleys which they rolled outside where they transferred their contents to larger wagons. When they saw Werner and Goldflame, they quickly brought up a couple of armchairs covered in gold brocade, and Goldflame said: "Let us sit down and watch the parade."

So they sat down and hardly a minute had passed before they heard a military band playing underneath one of the cupboards, and an entire Prussian regiment marched out and paraded before them in time to the music. Werner had never seen such marvellous lead soldiers. How smartly the little fellows lifted their legs and were saluted by their tiny officers' pin-like swords! Then came the regiments of horse with their shining breastplates, the lancers with their brightly coloured pennants, the Blue Dragoon Guards, and, last of all, the gun-carriages drawn by teams of horses. When all these had marched past, there was a "Tally ho!" from beneath the cupboard, and out streamed stags, hares and foxes followed by a pack of baying hounds and the huntsmen in red coats mounted on colourful horses and accompanied by the sound of hunting-horns and the cracking of whips. After this, fine snow suddenly began to fall. When the floor of the hall was white with it, a sleighing party appeared to the merry sound of sleigh-bells, and dashed past at speed. The fronts of the sleighs were made to resemble swans, lions, tigers and dragons, and tiny ladies and gentlemen dressed in fine furs rode in them, and threw little snowballs at the children as they passed by. But the snowballs didn't melt, for they were made out of boiled sugar wrapped in rice-paper.

The snow disappeared, and shepherds and shepherdesses walked past with their flocks to the melodious sound of cowbells. Then came little gardeners with fruit and flowers, gypsies, musicians, tight-rope walkers, and last of all a big travelling circus complete with caravans, giraffe, elephant, hippopotami, rhinoceros, zebra and antelope. The lions and panthers followed in cages on wheels, and roared like anything, small as they were.

When the parade was over, the two children mounted their horses and rode on. It was amazing how many things Werner saw: the Great Hall of Dolls, which didn't interest him particularly, but which made him wish that Anna could see it; the Theatre Shop where Goldflame ordered a hundred toy theatres to enact a hundred different plays all at the same time, which caused endless noise and confusion; the store-rooms for Meccano sets and building-blocks, for musical instruments, wooden animals, picture-books, paint-boxes, candles etc. etc. At last, when he was quite exhausted, they came to the Marzipan Warehouse.

"Now we will eat," said Goldflame. At once a table was

brought by six little pastry-cooks in white jackets and aprons and big white caps, and they swiftly set many delicious dishes before the children such as Werner had never seen or tasted the like of. There were marzipan birds stuffed with nougat, sausages made out of quince preserve, pink sugar ham, tartlets filled with strawberry jam and countless kinds of crystallised fruits. They drank pineapple juice with vanilla ice on top, and all the time the six little pastry-cooks stood by ready to serve them. The meal ended with particularly good black bread and delicious soft cheese. After this, the horses were brought round, and Goldflame said: "Now we will go and look over the mines." So they remounted, and their splendid steeds carried them out of the nearest door.

5 *The Mines*

They rode through fields where the most exquisite fruits and vegetables grew, all of which were made of marzipan, icing sugar or chocolates with soft centres; they galloped through great alley-ways lined with fruit-trees towards the mountains which lay before them. Some of the steep, rocky slopes were white as though made of chalk, but most were very dark and looked like black basalt. But all their summits were white and glistening as though covered in snow.

"I suppose you think that that is snow?" said Goldflame. "But when it snows here, it always snows castor sugar."

At last Werner saw a great, shining white cliff-face before him on which hundreds of workers were wielding hammers and pickaxes. "This is the Sugar Quarry," said Goldflame. "This whole mountainside is composed of the very best quality sugar!"

Close by, the entrance to a cave could be seen, and when the children approached it, several of the mining folk ran up and lit torches to show them the way. They penetrated into the very heart of the mountain where the walls shone dazzlingly in the torch-light, and suddenly they stepped out into an enormous cave whose walls were thickly covered in huge crystals of sugar candy.

"This is the Great Candy Cave," said Goldflame. They walked through it and came to a place where the miners were hammering and digging new tunnels in the mountain.

"They are looking for melted sugar," said Goldflame. "It is something like treacle, and is found in great hollows in this part of the mountain. When the miners find one of these, they dig the syrup out with long wooden spoons."

As they walked on, the mountain suddenly changed from being white and shining to a dull-looking dark brown colour, and began to smell of vanilla. "We are entering the chocolate area," said Goldflame.

Here there were many miners at work, and they had dug out the inside of the mountain until it looked like a salt-mine, and only a few columns were left here and there to support the roof. The finest vanilla chocolate could be found only in the centre of the mountain; the open workings yielded only bitter cooking chocolate. As they came out into the open air at last, Werner noticed a swift stream which flowed out of a gorge in the mountainside and rushed down into the valley, where it was used to drive water-mills which pounded the chocolate blocks into flat bars.

"Would you like a drink?" asked Goldflame. "This water tastes as good as the best brandy." All the sweet things he had eaten had made Werner very thirsty, and such a fresh, tempting aroma rose from the stream that he

took the cup of water which one of the miners handed him, and drained it at a gulp. But hardly had he emptied it than the world began to turn around him in the oddest way: he saw two, four, a hundred Goldflames which flickered and sparkled before his eyes and finally melted into one bright light, and on this golden flood he drifted off into unconsciousness.

6 *The End*

The first sound that little Werner heard when he came to his senses was the chirping of a blue-tit. He realised in astonishment that he was sitting on the tree-stump under the old beech, and before him was the little fir-tree. The blue-tit chirped and hopped about among its twigs as she had done before, only now he could no longer understand what she was trying to say. Then she flew up and disappeared into the topmost branches of the beech-tree. Werner realised in dismay that it must be evening-time, and that his mother must have been anxiously waiting for him to come home. But when he looked up at the sky, he saw to his surprise that – judging by the position of the sun – scarcely a quarter of an hour could have passed since he had set off on his travels. He couldn't think of any explanation for this, but he was so anxious to tell his mother and Anna about his strange adventure that he quickly chopped down the little fir-tree, and carried it home as fast as he could go.

When he had told her everything, his mother was quite cross, for she said that this was hardly the time of year to fall asleep in the forest. If it had been any colder, he could have caught his death. Then she shook her head and thought to herself:

"How does the boy dream up such extraordinary things?"

But Anna ran after him when he went out, crying, because his mother did not believe him, and questioned him tirelessly. In particular she wanted him to describe Goldflame and the Hall of Dolls over and over again, so that he took heart and repeated the whole story over from the beginning. During the days that followed he had to tell it countless times, and they even went into the wood to find the place where the door to the wonderful country had been. But although they reached the spot where the stream emerged from a marshy meadow, they could not find one place which was even vaguely like Werner's description, so that he felt quite confused and ashamed as he stood before Anna, unable to explain himself.

At last it was Christmas Eve. It had snowed heavily two days before, so that the world looked very Christmassy as it was supposed to. Darkness had fallen, and the children were sitting expectantly in the dark, whispering, and listening to their mother as she put the final touches to the decorations in the living-room, laid the few presents under the tree, and got ready to call the children in. Suddenly a sound like sleigh-bells could be heard in the distance, and it drew nearer and nearer, punctuated by the cracking of a whip. Now it was quite close, and then it stopped, and there were horses right outside the house; they were stamping their hooves in the snow, and when they shook their heads there was a faint tinkle of bells.

"Father Christmas! It is Father Christmas!" shouted Werner. They heard the door open, and a man's voice speaking, and suddenly their mother cried: "Children, come in! Your uncle is here!"

Werner and Anna ran into the room and saw a man in a big fur coat who held both arms out to them and shouted:

"Come here, children!" Then he lifted them up and kissed them one after another and said: "I want you to come and live with me in my big house in town. I will be a father to you, and bring you up to be useful and happy human beings." While this was going on, an enormous coachman with a fur cap, a long white beard and a coat with seven collars, kept coming in and out laden with large parcels. When these were opened, they contained a number of wonderful presents; never before had the children known such a Christmas Eve celebration. When they were finally in bed, Werner whispered to Anna: "You know who the coachman in the fur cap with the long white beard and the big coat was? It was Father Christmas. I recognised him at once, and he winked at me to prove it!"

But what had made their rich old uncle, who had lived a lonely and miserly existence and never bothered about his poor sister and her children, suddenly change into their benefactor?

In the night following the day when Werner visited Father Christmas, his uncle had had a strange dream. A man wearing a blue velvet cap and a long white beard suddenly stood before him dressed in a golden gown, fixed him for what seemed a long time with powerful blue eyes, and said very slowly and clearly:

"Conrad Borodin, do you have a sister?" At this, he was overcome by such a feeling of fear that he could not speak. Then the vision slowly faded: only the eyes continued to stare at him sternly. This dream repeated itself for three nights. In the meantime, he was driven by a feeling of extreme restlessness to wander about his bleak and empty house all day, and the deep, accusing voice of the dream-visitor kept ringing in his ears. Finally, on the fourth morning, he drove into town, and to the amazement of everyone who knew him for the miser he had been, he bought a great number of expensive gifts, hired a sleigh into which his coachman helped him to load them, and off they drove to his poor sister's house.

Little Werner became a famous and respected man, and it was he himself who told me this story.

The Snake-King

ONCE UPON A TIME there were three little girls whose job was to look after the geese. They tended them by the side of a pool which lay near the forest in the midst of green meadowland, where a few mighty oak-trees cast their cool shade in the heat of noon. Two of these girls were the daughters of wealthy peasants and the geese they looked after belonged to their fathers: they wore good clothes and clean white aprons, knitted stockings and real leather shoes and had embroidered caps on their heads. But the third girl was the only child of a poor widow, and she had to go barefoot all summer long. Although her dress was clean, it was made out of poor material and had been patched in many places, and over it she wore a grey hessian apron, while her head was covered with a faded blue kerchief. She was a quiet, modest and very pretty child, but the other girls treated her badly, for they thought themselves superior to the "Beggar-Girl" – as they called her – because of their smart clothes and wealthy fathers; and the only time they were friendly to her was when they needed her help. For she was very good at everything she did; the geese of the peasant who lived beside the pool were her responsibility, and they were the biggest and fattest in the whole village; she was very clever with her hands, too, so much so that the other village children used to say: "Goose-Greta can do anything!" She had a generous and helpful nature as well, and even when the other two had been so unkind to her that she had had to hide from them to shed bitter tears, she was always ready to unravel their tangled knitting for them, or plait their hair, or help them in any way she could, though she got no thanks for it. However much they mocked and teased her, however badly they treated her, she was always ready to forgive them, and was happy when they allowed her to be near them or to do anything for them.

One day, the two peasants' daughters were lying asleep in the shade of one of the big oak-trees out of the heat of the noonday sun, while Greta was left to tend the geese. She had taken her knitting to the edge of the wood, and was sitting by the pool whose banks, at this point, were steep, dry and sandy. There were only a few blades of grass here, but heather and wild thyme grew in profusion forming round, springy cushions that gave out a sweet, heady scent. Everything seemed to be sleeping in the hot sunshine; the silence was broken only by the drowsy humming of the honey-bees when suddenly Greta thought she could hear another sound, like a faint rustling noise in the dry grass. She waited as the sound drew nearer, keeping her eyes fixed on the sandy ground, when she saw a bright light flashing among the grass-stalks: to her astonishment it emanated from a little golden crown which sat upon the head of a white snake! The creature raised itself a little, peering from side to side with its cunning little eyes, but it did not notice Greta. Then it slid away behind a bush of thyme, and when it reappeared, the crown was no longer on its head. The snake wriggled down the bank to the water where it swam happily about and disappeared from view.

Greta would have liked to have had a look to see what had become of the golden crown, but she did not dare for

fear that the snake might come back. And sure enough, it reappeared after a while, came up the bank again, and disappeared into the flowering thyme. When it came out, it was wearing the crown once more, and moved rapidly away through the grass towards the wood.

When Greta told the other girls what she had seen, one of them said: "That was the Snake-King. My grandmother told me that he always takes off his crown before going for a swim. She said that anyone who discovers his bathing-place should lay a white cloth or apron on the ground, for he loves to put his crown down on something white. Once he has put it down, it must be picked up and carried off as fast as possible and across a stream or river. For the Snake-King cannot cross running water, and as soon as he notices that the crown has gone, he will whistle up all the snakes in the neighbourhood so that they may help to catch the thief. Anyone who steals the crown and does not reach safety in time may meet with an unpleasant end."

Early next morning, the girls washed their aprons in the pool and dried them in the sun, for they had decided to try to get hold of the Snake-King's crown. Around midday, the two farmers' daughters spread their snow-white aprons on the ground near the flowering thyme, but when Greta wanted to lay her rough grey apron beside theirs, they would not let her, and asked her mockingly whether she really imagined that the Snake-King would put his crown down upon such an ugly old grey rag. Weeping quietly to herself, Greta went away and spread her apron so far from the pool's edge that she had little hope of the snake even seeing it. Then they all three hid in the bushes, and waited.

It was not long before there was a rustling sound in the thin grass which got nearer and nearer. Soon the Snake-

King appeared. When he saw the two white aprons, he slithered up to them and examined the one that lay nearest to him, flicking his forked tongue rapidly in and out. He did not seem to like this apron and slid over it to the next one, which he examined as before. However, it did not please him either, for he moved away from it, curled up and sunned himself for a while. Suddenly he lifted his head high, for one of the little girls had made a slight noise: and as he looked all around, he caught sight of the third apron, and immediately began to wriggle towards it through the grass. Although it was only poor Greta's rough grey apron that lay there, the snake seemed to take the greatest pleasure in it, for he rolled and wriggled upon it, and finally put his crown down upon it and slid down into the pool, where he soon disappeared from view.

Greta jumped up, threw the apron over the flashing crown and shouted: "Come on quickly, before it is too late!"

At this, the other girls emerged sulkily from the bushes, took up their aprons, and followed her. But the Snake-King shot up out of the water like an arrow and began such a high, piercing whistle that it penetrated the whole wood. As the girls began to run towards the fresh-water spring whose shallow stream trickled down towards the pool, a terrifying rustling and hissing came from every direction as hundreds of snakes hurried through grass and heathland at their king's command. But the girls were able to jump over the spring just in time, and so they escaped the crownless king's revenge.

Now when the other girls were able to examine the stolen treasure, and could see how beautifully the delicate little crown was wrought, and that it had in its centre a sparkling blue jewel which looked as though it might be rather valuable, they were angrier and more envious than before, and would gladly have talked the happy Greta out of her treasure. But despite her obedient and generous nature, the little girl stood up to all their threats, pleading and flattery. Even when one of the girls offered her her gold Sunday chain with its coral locket and the other promised her her ring with the pale blue stone in return for the crown, she only shook her head and held her hand tightly over the pocket in which she had hidden her prize. They went on trying to get round her until evening came, and it was time to drive in the geese, but they achieved nothing, and had to go home without the crown.

The poor widow was delighted when Greta showed her what she had brought home with her. "That is a marvellous treasure," she said: "now we shall not be poor any more." When they had spent an hour or more admiring the delicate thing and turning it about in the lamplight to make it flash and sparkle, they wrapped it up carefully and shut it away in a chest. After that, mother and daughter went to bed. In the night they were both awakened by a soft whistling, and were astonished to see that the room was filled with a gentle light, although there was no moon. They saw that the light came from the Snake-King, who lay upon the floor giving out a phosphorescent glow, as though he were composed of moonbeams. He lifted up his head and said, in a fine, silvery voice: "Give me back my little crown and I will reward you handsomely! A rare flower will grow in your garden, the like of which you have never seen. If you dig in the place in which it appears, you will find a great treasure. I do not ask you to return my crown until you have seen this promise fulfilled. But if, after that, you do not obey my wish, a terrible misfortune will befall you."

When the Snake-King had spoken these words, he glided behind the stove and disappeared.

Greta and her mother could sleep no more that night, full as they were with excitement and impatience. The day had scarcely dawned before they were in the dew-drenched garden searching for the promised flower. But although they looked everywhere, they could find nothing unusual, and were just about to give up when suddenly, just as the first rays of the sun rose above the horizon, a strange, melodious ringing filled the air, and a spice-laden aroma permeated the whole garden. At the same instant, the earth beneath a big apple-tree opened a little, and a shining green shoot shot up through the crack; its leaves unfurled even as they watched, and from its centre sprang a stalk bearing three golden buds. The ringing became louder and the aroma stronger until suddenly the buds burst open and three flowers appeared; each was an exact replica of the Snake-King's crown, and each also had a jewelled centre that shone like a blue star. But hardly had it attained perfect maturity before each flower hung its lovely head, and soon only a poor, withered plant stood there, all brown and dead.

The woman began to dig at the place where the magic flower had appeared, and soon she unearthed a large pot which was filled to the brim with gold coins and precious stones, so that she became a rich woman in an instant. Greta returned the crown to the Snake-King on the very same day. But her mother, who told no one about the discovery of the buried treasure, soon sold her little property to a neighbouring peasant who had long wanted to add it to his farm, and moved with Greta to a distant town where they lived in great comfort in a pretty house with a garden. She sent her daughter to a very good school where she learned many things, and the little goose-girl grew into a clever and beautiful young woman, who later married a handsome man of good family.

And so these two founded a flourishing and well-to-do

family, whose descendants still exist today, and whose coat-of-arms contains a silver snake with a crown on its head, and two golden geese.

The Three Sisters

ONCE THERE WAS a man who had three daughters. The first was called Armynel, and was a proud and haughty character. Her hair was black with a bluish tinge like a raven's wing, and her skin was white and as smooth as ivory; when she walked through the streets in a dignified manner dressed in beautiful clothes, the people stared after her and called her the "Black Princess". Sylvia, the second daughter, had brown hair, and she looked upon the world out of laughing eyes, as gay as a morning in early spring. She danced more than she walked, so that her plaits and ribbons flew about. The third daughter was called Freda; she had a quiet, unassuming nature and passed almost unnoticed when her sisters were present. True, her hair was a very unusual colour, and shone like spun gold when the sunlight caught it; but the delicate skin of her face was covered with freckles like a bird's egg, and as she dressed very simply and walked about silently and pensively, she was totally eclipsed by her sisters' personalities and no one bothered about her very much. While the other two were concerned with their appearances and their pursuit of pleasurable distractions, she did the housekeeping and busied herself calmly and noiselessly in kitchen and house like a good fairy.

But it happened that the father fell so seriously ill that even the cleverest doctors despaired of his life, and even though they prescribed the most elaborate and expensive medicines, and frowned and twiddled their ivory-tipped walking-sticks, they could not think of a cure for his illness. The poor man languished and grew ever weaker, and if help did not soon come, it was clear that he must die.

In a neighbouring wood, a spring burst out of a dark ravine which was supposed to be inhabited by a Water Monster. It was said that the water of the spring, if drawn from its very source, had the power to heal even the most terrible illnesses. The gravity of their father's condition reminded the girls of this legend, and the eldest made preparations to go and fetch some of the water. She took the beautiful silver jug with its gold decorations – an old family heirloom – and walked off towards the wood. She was magnificently dressed in silk and gold brocade and hung about with valuable jewellery, and as she walked, such a rustling of skirts and clinking of ornaments emanated from her that the birds looked down from the trees in astonishment. In this manner, she reached the Water Monster's spring, and proudly announced to him the reason for her journey.

He looked strangely at her out of small, green eyes, and said: "I will give you the water if you will be my wife. There is a cave in the cliff where you can rest on soft moss, and I will protect and care for you faithfully."

Armynel stared at the Water Monster with undisguised disgust, for she regarded his request as both impudent and totally out of the question. And it must be admitted that he was certainly no beauty. His wide mouth was full of green pointed teeth, and matted blue-green hair hung about his bronzed face like reed-grass. His whole body was covered with thick hair, like an otter's, and he had ugly webbed fingers with sharp claws, so that his hands resembled those of a frog. Armynel's eyes looked beyond him to the walls of the dark gorge, and saw the water dripping down them, and the long green algae that hung from them like the monster's hair; and she forgot all about her father pining away on his bed of sickness; all she could think of was that she should have to live in this dark, damp place at the side of the hideous monster, far from the light of the sun and the splendour of life in a society in which people constantly gazed at her with undisguised admiration.

"Never," she said, looking at the Water Monster with a proud and hostile expression.

"I thought as much," said he, and he grinned so that his mouth stretched from one ear to the other, and all his green, pointed teeth were visible. "But," he went on, "it is not proper that such a fine, proud lady should travel on foot; I will lend you a horse that shall carry you home."

With this, he reached into the bottom of the spring, fetched up a smooth, black pebble, and threw it into the air. Even before it touched the ground, a shining black horse stood there; its behaviour was quiet and demure, and it pawed the ground delicately.

Armynel's eyes sparkled, for she adored riding. She looked at the Water Monster in an almost friendly way and bestowed a condescending smile upon him when he approached and helped her courteously into the saddle. At first the black horse trotted quietly along through the gorge: but suddenly there was a deafening noise of clapping hands, and the voice of the Water Monster yelled: "Ho, ho, Courser! Hey, ho!" until the cliff-walls echoed and re-echoed.

At this, the horse seemed possessed of the devil himself. First it stood upon its hind legs for a while, and then it put its head down and galloped off until its rider didn't know whether she was coming or going. Away through the wood it rushed, through bramble-thickets and low-hanging branches, until silk, gold brocade and jewels hung in shreds upon the thorn-bushes or were for ever lost, and the girl's face was all scratched and bleeding. Then it took off across a sandy field full of thistles, so that a cloud of dust flew out in its wake; from there, it galloped down the bank into the river until the water closed over both their heads; and on and on, across meadows and marshland, until finally the demoniac steed stopped with a sudden jerk in front of her father's house, dug its forefeet into the ground, shot the girl over its head into the sand, and vanished without a trace. Later, a neighbour's little boy found a smooth black pebble where the girl had landed. But when he carried it down to the spring to wash the dust off it, it slid out of his hand, and he could not find it anywhere.

The next day Sylvia, the second daughter, went out to try her luck with the Water Monster. She wore a dress of silver taffeta decorated with thousands of spangles and coloured ribbons, and as a receptacle for the water she took along a very fragile and valuable Venetian glass vase. She skipped along through the wood, and her be-ribboned plaits bobbed up and down in time with her light feet. When she got to the Water Monster's spring, she made a curtsey, and told him her errand. When she received the same reply as her sister, the whole idea seemed to her so ridiculous that she could hardly keep a straight face. She, too, forgot her father who lay dying on his bed of suffering – longing for the healing water – so she laughed out loud in the Water Monster's face. Then she lifted up her dress with the tips of her fingers, twirled gracefully before him so that her petticoats flew, and said: "That is just what you would like, you old grizzly bear! But you won't get it. A funny sight that would be, if I went dancing with an old Flipper-foot like you!"

The Water Monster grinned as before, so that his mouth stretched from one ear to the other, and said: "I thought as much. But I see that you are fond of dancing. I will give you the best partner in the world, the Whirlwind himself!"

"No, I don't want to: I won't dance with him!" cried Sylvia. But the Water Monster had already taken a deep breath and blown it forth into the air, where it turned into a twisting, twirling, invisible thing which seized Sylvia round the waist. Then the Water Monster whistled shrilly through his fingers, and splashed some water from the spring around. "Ho, ho! Dance, my Poppet! Hey, ho!" he cried. At this, the invisible grip on Sylvia's waist tightened, and she was whirled away, so that dust and dry leaves flew, and the trees roared as they rushed by. Oh, that was a dance through woods and meadows, across the heath and through the fast-flowing river! And the whirling wind drew thunder and lightning after it and pouring rain, until Sylvia was left lying breathless and exhausted and with her clothes soaking wet and in tatters on the threshold of her father's house, having had her fill of dancing.

The next day at noon, Freda was the last to go and try her luck with the Water Monster. She had put on a clean white dress, and carried a brown earthenware jug carefully in her hand. It was very hot as the sun reached its zenith; all the birds were silent, and the whole wood was asleep. Even the little stream which ran out of the gorge and then disappeared into the earth again between some rocks murmured as drowsily as though it were talking in its sleep. Freda stepped out of the sultry air of the wood into the cool dampness of the gorge, and walked on over the mossy ground. Ancient pine-trees stretched out their dark branches to one another high above, so that only a tiny patch of blue sky showed here and there. As she neared the bottom of the gorge, the cliffs rose higher and higher on either side, and at last she came to the Water Monster's spring. This resembled a shell of stone over whose edges the water flowed evenly into a second, shallower basin, and this in turn overflowed into a narrow channel running between blocks of stone that lay upon the ground. She could hear nothing except the murmuring of the spring and the dripping and gurgling sounds the water made as it ran down the mossy cliff-face.

Suddenly she started, for she saw a hairy creature, somewhat resembling a man, lying against the cliff behind the basin into which the spring emptied itself. It was the Water Monster, sleeping quietly, as he hung his webbed frog's feet over the edge of the basin into the water. A shiver ran through her at seeing the hideous monster at such close quarters. She stood there for a little while, waiting for him to wake up. But, when he slept on, she took a pebble and threw it into the stream. And what a fright she got when he suddenly jumped up and stared at her out of his small, yellow-green eyes.

"Not another one!" he exclaimed. "What do YOU want of me?"

Freda shyly told him what she had come for, and got the same answer as her sisters. Now she shuddered anew, but she remembered her pale, dying father, and said: "I will gladly become your wife if you will only cure my father."

"I thought as much," he said. And he smiled all over his face. It was astonishing to see how nice he could look.

Then he reached down into the water of the spring, and fished out an emerald jug, full to the brim with the life-giving water, and handed it to the girl. When she had thanked him and was turning to go, he said: "Wait a moment!", reached into the water again, and sprinkled her hair and dress with it; and lo and behold, all these drops of water turned into shining pearls and sparkling diamonds,

so that Freda looked like a princess. Then he stroked her face gently, and said: "Now look into the water." To her great joy, Freda's face looked back at her from the clear water all smooth and velvet-skinned and free of ugly freckles. Next, the Water Monster took three pebbles out of the stream, laid them on the ground, and murmured a few strange words over them while he sprinkled them with water. The stones immediately turned into milk-white horses which were harnessed to a shining carriage of ivory and mother-of-pearl. When Freda had climbed into it, the horses trotted away in great style, while the Water Monster played upon his golden harp and sang so beautifully that it was astonishing to hear such lovely tones coming out of so hideous a body.

Armynel and Sylvia had been sitting at the window for quite a while, because they were maliciously looking forward to seeing their youngest sister returning with an empty jug and in a state of total disarray. But great was their amazement when a shining wonder suddenly appeared round the corner; it sparkled and flashed in the sunlight, and a green star shone from its centre. This was the emerald jug containing the water of life which Freda was holding on her lap. When the strange conveyance stopped at the door of the house and Freda stepped out of it, horses and carriage disappeared, and only three shining pebbles lay upon the sand.

Freda carried the beautiful jug into her father's room, and as soon as she entered it, the room was filled with the scent of spring flowers and vintage wine. The sick man raised himself in bed, and the colour crept into his cheeks again. He reached for the emerald jug with both hands and took a long draught of renewed health, strength and life, and the sickness left him then and there.

When the two sisters saw this, and the lovely clothes

and jewels that Freda was wearing caught their envious eyes, and they realised that she was now much more beautiful to look upon than a real princess, their anger and jealousy knew no bounds, and they mocked and made fun of her because she had promised to marry the Water Monster, and nicknamed her the Frog Queen. But Freda took it very calmly and did not argue with them. The following night, however, when dawn was already breaking and Freda was lying in bed in her little room, unable to sleep for the thoughts that crowded in upon her, she suddenly heard a knock on the outer door, and a voice called out:

"O lovely girl, get up and dress!
Your bridegroom stands outside the house."

Freda was very frightened, and pretended she had not heard anything. But then she heard the front door open, and from the passage below, a voice called:

"O lovely girl, put on your shawl!
Your bridegroom stands within the hall."

But she still did not move. Then she heard a heavy step upon the stairs, as of feet wearing flippers, and a voice called out:

"O lovely girl, put up your hair!
Your bridegroom is upon the stair."

With this, there was a knock on the bedroom door, and so Freda got out of bed and opened it. Outside stood the Water Monster in all his ugliness. "I have come to remind you of your promise," he said, "and to take you away with me."

"I am ready," said the girl, although her heart was trembling in horror.

Then the Water Monster smiled as kindly as he could, and said: "Wash me first!"

"I will do as you say, Master," replied Freda. And she fetched some water, and began to wash him. But wherever the water touched him, the otter-pelt fell away from him, and soon a beautiful young man was standing before her, dressed in sea-green silk, and so handsome that her heart was on fire with love for him. He led her down the stairs to the door of the house. Outside stood a golden coach drawn by silver-white horses; footmen in blue liveries opened the carriage door, and away they went at a smart trot.

The dark gorge had turned itself into a beautiful garden full of rushing springs and spouting fountains, and in its centre stood a castle whose beauty must surely have been unequalled. There they lived for many years, had lovely children, and all was happiness and harmony.

But Armynel and Sylvia were so annoyed and jealous that they got jaundice, and lost all their good looks. So, in the course of time, they became two ugly old maiden aunts.

The Timepiece

ONCE THERE WAS an old clock which was tired of ticking away all the time. It was so poorly of late that its strike had become hoarse and indistinct, rather like the voice of a toothless old man; and when it struck, such a rumbling and whirring came from its inside that it was easy to see how sick of the whole business of keeping time it had become. "Something is wrong with my works," it said to itself, "it is probably the rheumatics."

Day by day its weariness increased: finally, it couldn't go on any longer. "Time goes quicker than I do," it said, "and what is the use of my trying to run after it?" And with that, it stopped. So it was taken to the clock-doctor. He poked around inside it with his pointed tools and peered through his magnifying glass at the most intimate parts of its interior, shook his head and said to the father of little Hal, whose clock it was: "There is nothing to be done. It is old age. I might be able to get it to go for a little while longer, but it can never really be put right. It would be better for you to buy a new one."

So that is what was done. A very imposing-looking, highly polished clock joined the household; it called itself by an outlandish foreign name meaning "The Timepiece", and it made one feel as though it expected to be addressed as "Sir". Its appearance, grave and dignified and rather pompous as it was, reminded one of a senior civil servant; it kept accurate time, and had such a loud voice that its strike could be heard through the entire house. It possessed, in addition, a huge inner strength, so that it only needed to be wound up every fortnight, whereas the old clock would have run down if it had been overlooked for just one day.

But the old clock was such a pretty old clock, and so mother said to little Hal: "Even if it is old and wobbly and no longer goes, it is nonetheless very decorative." And so the clock kept its accustomed place on top of the silver-cupboard. But father said: "It is pensioned off and has gone into retirement, which it richly deserves. It was present at my father's birth and at my grandfather's funeral, and it struck the hour at which I led your mother to the altar. It is a member of the family."

When little Hal heard this, and his father had gone away, he stood thoughtfully looking up at the clock. He had never really noticed how pretty it was. The upper part in which the clock-face lay was made of dark wood and stood upon four pillars of shining alabaster; these in their turn rested upon a black pediment ornamented with brass. A golden eagle perched on the very top, and on each side of the clock-case stood two gilded female figures, blowing on trumpets. Between the pillars, there was a little hall with plateglass walls in which stood a shining statuette of a woman wearing a helmet and breastplate; she held a burning torch in one hand and a spear in the other, while a shield hung over one forearm. She represented the Roman goddess, Minerva. The brass pendulum of the clock was made to look like a round face encircled by rays – like the sun. The more Hal looked at the old clock the more sorry he was that it was so still and speechless, and he felt as though it had actually died. While he was still standing there, he suddenly heard the brisk voice of the Timepiece where it hung on the opposite wall, saying: "Tick-tock: snick-snerks: clicker-clack."

He looked at it in astonishment as it began again: "Tick-tock: snick-snerks: clicker-clack." After which, it gave out loud whirrings and clinkings which sounded very much like unpleasant, mocking laughter. At this it seemed that a pathetic, trembling ring came out of the old clock; Hal could not tell what had caused it: perhaps the vibrations from a passing carriage? But he found it moving in the extreme.

Since then, he had conceived a special love for the old clock and would often stand and look at it and dream. But for the moment, the Timepiece did nothing out of the ordinary.

When relatives came to stay with Hal's parents, he had to sleep in the room where the clocks stood as the flat was rather small. After he had gone to bed on the sofa, he lay awake for a while, for he was unused to the loud ticking of the Timepiece and it would not let him sleep. As he lay listening to the hard, regular sound of the pendulum he noticed a strange change taking place in it, and soon it had altered its rhythm to what sounded like: "Tick-tock: snick-snerks: clicker-clack" and, just as before, it followed this up with a noise like laughter. And the old clock gave out a soft, sad sound. When little Hal tried to listen to see if the Timepiece would repeat its odd little song, he fell asleep instead.

He was awakened by the Timepiece loudly striking midnight, and saw to his astonishment that the whole room was brightly lit. Could the moon be shedding so much light? But before he could find out, he was doubly amazed to hear the familiar, hoarse voice of the old clock striking twelve too. He was just going to sit up and look around at it when he saw a bright figure, all shining gold, standing beside his bed. It was the Minerva out of the old clock, only now she was as tall as a grown-up person. She carried her spear, shield and torch, and bowed to Hal as she said:

"The old clock would like to speak with you."

Little Hal was about to put on his clothes when he realised that he was already dressed in his best blue-velvet Sunday suit. He jumped out of bed and saw that a strange transformation had taken place in the room. It had turned into a large hall at the end of which the old clock stood, but it, too, had grown enormously. It now looked like a small palace, and the light that Hal had noticed before came from the swinging pendulum which not only shone like the sun but was reflected back from the mirror-glass walls as well. The shining golden Minerva walked in front of Hal, her armour ringing as she went, and as they drew nearer, the two statues on either side of the clock-face blew a mighty blast on their trumpets and the eagle flapped his wings and turned around three times. A flight of steps which Hal had not noticed before led up to the pediment. They climbed up it and found themselves in the entrance-hall with the mirror-glass walls; the gold pendulum swung back and forth directly over their heads. On a signal from Minerva, the mirrors at the end of the hall folded back like two doors, and beyond them there appeared yet another hall in which an old man with a grey beard sat sadly at a table with his chin in his hand. Hal walked in, and the doors closed behind him.

The old man lifted his head wearily, looked with dim eyes at the little boy, and spoke in a weak voice: "I am glad that you have come: oh, if only you were able to lighten my sorrow!" Little Hal did not know what to say: he stared at the old man with wondering eyes. But the latter went

on mournfully: "I am the Spirit of the Clock: the clock and I are one and the same. We did our duty throughout many long years by your great-grandparents, your grandparents and lastly by your father and mother. We indicated to them all their sad and happy hours and never tired, as long as a little strength remained to us, of telling them the time. But steel and metal are perishable: they, too, fall victim to the inexorable passage of Time. Our limbs have grown old and feeble and our voice has become hoarse and faint. What you see up there," – and he pointed upwards to where the rusty old wheels were turning laboriously – "is only the brief dream-life of a ghost. Your father meant well when he retired us from active life, but at the same time, he added a new torment to our existence to which we are subjected day and night. For he hung that modern, polished upstart on the opposite wall, whose mocking talk reminds us constantly of his superior, brutal strength. Listen! He is repeating those cruel words which cut us to our innermost cog-wheels!"

Hal heard the voice of the Timepiece outside: "Tick-tock: snick-snerks: clicker-clack!"

A deep, sighing breath seemed to fill the hall, and the old man went on: "You do not understand what those words mean. I will tell you: Tick-tock is a working clock: snick-snerks, it no longer works: clicker-clack, it is bric-à-brac! – and then away with it on to the nearest rubbish-heap. We might be able to bear the insult if it were not repeated every day and followed by mocking laughter: as it is, we are deeply hurt by it. We may be nothing but old rubbish, but if so, we would rather be relegated to the attic where we belong and where we would not be exposed to the taunts of that brutal upstart. And it is because I want you to persuade your father to move us into the attic that I have sent for you. Once there, we shall at least find peace and quiet."

The old man fell silent, gasping with exhaustion. But then a strange light shone for an instant in his faded eyes, and he drew himself up a little as he said: "There is one other way to help us, but I fear that there is little hope that your father might consider it. This would be to have a new mechanism made for us, one that would be even more powerful than the one that polished wretch contains. All my limbs tremble with joy at the mere thought! But can there be any hope of it?"

So saying, he laid his weary old head upon the table and began to weep; then he seemed to fall asleep. At the same time, the hall grew dark, the sound of the clock became fainter and fainter, one last melancholy note floated through the hall, and then all was pitch-dark and silent.

Little Hal woke next morning at the usual time, sat up on his sofa-bed, and looked curiously about him, for he at once remembered the wonderful events of the night. But there was nothing unusual about the room. He got dressed, ran to his father, and told him everything that had happened, and begged him to have a lovely new mechanism made for the old clock. His father stared at him for a moment. Then he laughed and said: "Dear boy, however do you manage to dream up such a lot of rubbish? You must have been reading too many fairy-stories."

But little Hal swore that it had been no dream; he had really seen and experienced the whole thing. And he renewed his plea. Then his father got cross, and said: "I don't want to hear any more about it. Besides, the old, wobbly, rubbishy thing isn't worth a new mechanism. But because I see that your head is full of stuff and nonsense, I'll give you three sums to do to give you something else to think about!"

So Hal had to do sums all day, even though it was holiday-time, because they were so difficult that he could not get them finished until supper-time. And the next day he had to do them all over again, because he had got all three answers wrong. And he wished he had never spoken about the night's adventure. However, the Spirit of the Clock's second wish was granted without any effort on Hal's part, for a grand and stuck-up aunt came by on a visit and happened to say to Hal's mother: "Really, Natalie, I can't understand how you can tolerate that old broken-down monstrosity on top of your silver-cupboard! The thing is completely out of fashion and belongs in the attic. But what a beautiful Timepiece you have got since I was last here!"

As she spoke these words, a satisfied whirring came from the interior of the Timepiece, and its pendulum made a vainer and more pompous sound than ever. But Hal's mother took the aunt's word for it, because she was so grand and lived in a fine town house and so must know what she was talking about. And the very same day, the old clock was put up in the attic, and in its place appeared a statue of a young woman who was supposed to represent Virtue or Wisdom or Knowledge or something of a moral nature, and was entirely made out of plaster.

After this, no one bothered about the old clock except Hal, who, long after he had reached the sixth form at school and had been known as Henry, used to go up to the attic to see his dear old exiled friend, dust it off and look at it for a while. He had long ago resolved to restore it to a respected position in his own household, and when he had become a well-known doctor of medicine and had a wife and a home of his own, he asked his parents for the old clock, had a fine new set of works made for it, and gave it the place of honour in his drawing-room. There it can be seen – and heard – to this very day. There is a new little Hal, too, who loves and respects it as once his father used to do.

But the Timepiece has become old and dilapidated, and has had to make room for a younger clock. It now hangs in the wash-house next to the kitchen, and goes all wrong, so that no one can rely upon it. Tick-tock: snick-snerks: clicker-clack!

Little Marie

ONCE THERE WAS a little girl whose name was Marie. Her father and mother were dead, and a horrid old man had taken her away, saying that he was her uncle. She lived with him in a big, wild forest. If this man came home from hunting and found that Marie had not cleaned and polished the whole cottage and cooked the supper and milked the cow, he scolded her, beat her, and gave her dry bread to eat.

Little Marie worked all day without stopping, but she was still too small and weak to do all that was expected of her. The old cow with the lovely white face was her only friend. Marie talked to her and stroked her and told her all her troubles, but of course the cow could not help her.

One evening the man had beaten her again, and sent her hungry to bed. There she lay in her little room and cried. The moon looked through the window, caressed her with his long beams, and shone upon her pillow.

"O, you dear moon," said little Marie: "please help me!" The good moon made a face, but it slid down from Marie's pillow and let a bright beam fall upon her bedspread. Marie nearly got a fright, for a snow-white mouse was sitting there and nodding its head at her. But Marie wasn't afraid of mice, as some little girls are, for when the old man was out, mice were her only playfellows, and she had often scattered a few breadcrumbs for them.

The mouse spoke quite clearly in a squeaky voice:
"Come with me, little Marie: we mice have resolved to help you; I will take you out into the beautiful forest and you shall live there with the little dwarfs."
"But how can I go with you?" said little Marie. "The door is locked, the windows have bars, and the fierce dog, whose job it is to see that I don't get out, is lying outside the door."
"We will go out through our house," said the mouse. "We have a front door of our own."
"Heavens!" said Marie: "through a mousehole? Then I would have to make myself thinner than a sausage!"
The white mouse gave a high whistle, and a coal-black mouse jumped on to the bed. It carried in its mouth a black root, which it laid before Marie.
"Eat that," said the white mouse, "and you will be as small as the smallest dwarf."
"Will it hurt?" asked little Marie.
"No, but it tastes nasty," said the mouse.
"Pooh!" said the little girl, making a face. The root tasted as sour as an unripe crab-apple, and made her pucker up her lips. Suddenly it seemed to her that she was floating above the ground, there was a humming and singing noise in her ears, and the whole room seemed to turn over. Then there was a jerk, and she was lying in her bed, as neat and as tiny as a wax doll.
"O mouse, where are you?" she cried, "and what is this mountain lying on top of me?"
The mouse looked down at her and squeaked with pleasure at the sight of the tiny creature.
"Here I am," it said, "and the mountain is your eider-down: now come, we must away."
"O mouse, I cannot get down!" cried little Marie as she

peered over the edge of the bed into the depths below.

"That is bad. I didn't think of that," said the mouse. But luckily a towel was hanging near the bedpost, and the white mouse took Marie's dress in its teeth and climbed down to the ground with her in its mouth.

"Oh, how dark it is!" said Marie. "Don't you have any lights here?"

"Be patient, Marie. Catch hold of my tail and take courage!"

The passageway was long and dark. It didn't smell very nice in there: but stale bacon-rind and mouldy cheese are like Parisian scent to mouse-noses.

After a while, it grew a little lighter: a moonbeam shone through a crack in the wall and lit up a fairly large room, or so it seemed to the now very little Marie. But in reality, it was no bigger than a box.

"This is the living-room," said the mouse. "You must stay here with us, little Marie, until it is daylight, otherwise you will never find your way through the forest."

There was a rustling and scampering and squeaking and scrabbling in the passageways so that Marie felt quite nervous. "Don't be afraid," said the white mouse. "There are a lot of wild goings-on here today, because we are giving a ball tonight and everything must be properly prepared: it makes a lot of work."

Great preparations were afoot in the drawing-room next door. Some mice were licking the walls so clean that they shone, while others polished the floor with tallow. Visiting field-mice came in from outside: they wore reddish-brown suits and white waistcoats. One of them rolled in a hollow walnut out of which it emptied a quantity of glow-worms.

"Oh, how they shine!" cried little Marie. The mice

arranged the glow-worms on ledges round the walls, and they had hung a few ears of corn from the middle of the ceiling on which they also placed a glow-worm or two.

"A good chandelier," said the white mouse. "When we have made good use of it, we can eat it."

"Does corn taste good?" asked Marie.

"I like candle-grease better," replied the mouse, "but that is a matter of personal taste. You shall sit here on this half-a-walnut shell, little Marie. The ball will start at any minute."

Now the whole room was festively lit: true, the light was not too bright, but it was possible to see, and mice have sharp eyes. High up in the wall there was an alcove, and in it sat the Music Mouse.

"This Music Mouse comes from the forest especially to make music," said the white mouse. "It gets twenty paw-fuls of candle-grease and four walnuts for the evening. It won't perform for less."

"Are you the Head Mouse?" asked little Marie.

"Yes I am," said the white mouse.

Now all the mice were ready, and the Music Mouse began to sing, almost like a bird twittering. Then the mice started to scurry here and there, all muddled up and topsy-turvy. It was a strange sort of dance.

"She sings very nicely," said little Marie.

"Yes: she has a good class squeak," said the white mouse.

The mice were scampering round the walls one moment and forming a tight knot in the centre of the room the next; sometimes they jumped at one another as though they meant to bite each other. But they were only pretending. And all the while, the twittering voice of the Music Mouse could be heard, and when Marie listened to it, she could understand the words of the song:

"Rustle, rustle, little mouse,
in and out and round and round – :
popping up from underground
through the hole-door to your house.
Scribble-scrabble near the floor;
mice can always find a door:
mice can slip through any crack
and can find a place to hide them
till the Cat pads up beside them!
Quietly the Cat draws near
waiting for them to appear.
Mice, oh mice, don't make a sound!
You are safest underground!
Hustle – hide!
The Cat's outside! . . ."

Suddenly all the mice had disappeared into their holes as though a cat were really there. But they popped up again one by one, and the dance began anew.

Little Marie thought this was great fun. She joined in the singing, and when the "hustle – hide!" came, she clapped her little hands as loudly as she could.

But now the mice were hungry from all the dancing they had done. A splendid supper was served: bacon-fat and mouldy cheese followed by a dessert of walnuts with candle-grease. Little Marie was given half a walnut for herself of which she ate a small piece, putting the rest in her pocket for the coming journey. The food had all gone, and the visiting mice had set off for their homes. Then the white mouse said:

"Now it is getting light, Marie, and we must go. I will accompany you myself, and take you to the good little dwarfs who live deep in the forest on the shores of Dwarf Lake; you will be quite safe there."

"Do I have to stay so very tiny?" asked little Marie.

"No," said the mouse. "The dwarfs know the root that can make you grow again."

They went along a dark passage which eventually came out under a pile of wood in the forest. The sun had risen and glistened in the dewdrops hanging from the blades of grass through which Marie and the mouse crept noiselessly, so as not to arouse the fierce dog. After a while, they came to a forest path and walked along it until they reached a stream that flowed through the forest.

"We must follow this stream for a while," said the mouse, "until we reach a place where a tree has fallen across it. There we shall be able to cross."

When they had been walking beside the water for a little while, they heard the sudden barking of a dog behind them.

"Oh dear!" cried little Marie, "now the man has noticed that I am missing, and has sent the fierce dog after us!"

And sure enough, the dog could be heard crashing through the undergrowth quite close behind them.

"Run and hide, Marie!" squeaked the white mouse. "I cannot help you now!" and in a moment, it had vanished.

Marie ran through the tall grass, hearing the dog sniffing almost at her heels, when all of a sudden she lost her footing and tumbled down the steep bank of the stream. The dog could be heard snuffling around up above, but he had lost the scent, and set up a dismal howling. Then the man caught up with him, cursed and beat him, and they both went away. Soon it was quiet once more. So the mouse emerged from its hiding-place and called: "Marie, Marie!" but no one answered.

"She must have fallen into the stream and been drowned," it thought, and went sadly home.

But little Marie was lying comfortably inside a water-lily, for she had tumbled straight into it, and was still too shaken from her fall to hear the mouse's voice.

When she came to her senses, she looked around in astonishment, for she thought she was lying in a golden bed with white walls, and she could see brightly coloured flowers and grass above her head, for these were nodding down at her from the banks of the stream where they grew. She sat up carefully – for the water-lily rocked when she moved – and peeped over the edge of the flower. But there was water all around her with high banks towering above it. More water-lilies floated nearby, and great, slender dragonflies danced in the air above. Suddenly she got a fright and ducked down inside the flower to hide from an enormous frog who sat on a flat leaf goggling with his big, shiny eyes. But he had already caught sight of her and – plop! – he jumped into the water and swam towards her. "Croak – croak!" he said: "What's that, what's that? Let's look, let's look!"

The water-lily rocked violently as the huge creature grabbed at its edge with its great green fingers. Marie was trembling with fear and bent quite double in her effort to become invisible when she heard a whirring sound above her, and a voice whispered: "Climb up, climb up, little girl, quickly – quickly!"

A big dragonfly was sitting on the edge of the lily: its transparent wings trembled as Marie climbed on to its back as fast as she could and whirr! they rose into the air. Plop! up jumped the frog from the water, opened his large mouth and stuck his long tongue out as far as it would go, but he could not reach them. "Croak – croak!" he said: "Silly folk playing pranks –: no thanks!" and he clambered back on to his leaf again.

The flight through the air was lovely, so swift and smooth and safe that Marie was not at all afraid.

"Dragonfly, where are we flying to?" she asked.

"To the island," said the dragonfly. "It has steep banks up which no frog can climb."

In the middle of the stream lay a large rock with steep, slippery sides. It was no bigger than a table, and covered in flowers, wild strawberries and bilberry bushes. Ferns, too, grew there, hanging their curly fronds over the water, and a tiny spruce-tree had rooted on the summit, where it looked like a doll's Christmas Tree. Here the dragonfly deposited little Marie saying: "Little girl, here you can make your home. Build yourself a little house under the tree."

"Thank you, kind dragonfly," said Marie. But the dragonfly had already risen, whirring, into the air, and was dancing away above the green leaves of the beech-trees.

Little Marie stayed on the island all summer long. She built a tiny house out of moss, grass and spiders' threads: the roof was so thick that no rain could come through, and her playfellows were butterflies, who came to call on her, and the little beetles which lived in the moss. When she grew hungry, she picked a strawberry – and this kept her nourished for the whole day. And if she felt thirsty, she would let a harebell-flower down into the stream on a spider's thread, and fetch up a drop of water. All the insects loved little Marie, and helped her in every way they could. She only had to put a leaf outside her door for a passing bee to place a drop of honey on it. The dragonflies were her winged carriages in which she rode above the green twigs in the warm sunshine. Once a very big, strong dragonfly had carried her right up over the forest trees, so that she could see tree-top upon tree-top and the endless forest stretching away below like a green sea. The big frog had swum downstream, and now lived on a nearby leaf and was quite friendly. Once she threw him a strawberry, but he only croaked at it, pushed it with his nose, and let it float away.

When the summer had reached its height, the strawberries were over, but the bilberries hung from their tiny trees like dark blue plums, and Marie's mouth was stained with their juice. Her clothes were in rags by now, so she sat under the fern-fronds and stitched some new ones together out of flower-petals. A dried harebell made a very pretty blue skirt. She sewed with a wasp-sting threaded with cobweb, and decorated her dresses with flies' wings and the coloured shells of beetles which she found lying about after they had discarded them for new ones. Upside-down on her head she sometimes wore a little red flower for a cap.

Then the autumn came, and the nights grew cold. But the sky was blue in the daytime, and the sun shone warmly down. One night, when the moon was shining brightly, little Marie woke in her petal-lined bed to the sound of sweet voices singing and laughing. She peeped out of her door and saw that the whole island was alive with dainty little people, no bigger than Marie herself, and light as a breath of air. They were dancing in a ring, and more and more joined them, riding on threads of gossamer – several to a thread. Marie could see them clearly in the bright moonlight. Suddenly they too saw her, and gathered round her.

"Who are you?" they asked. "Are you a dwarf?"

"No, no! She is a person – a real little person!" one of them cried.

Then a lovely young woman appeared who was probably their queen, for she wore a gold band round her hair, and all the others made room for her and treated her with great respect.

"How did you get here, little human child?" she asked.

Marie told her story.

"Would you like to come with us?" said the young woman.

"We are on our way to the warm countries in the South."

"Oh, I would!" said Marie, "for when the first snow falls, my legs will freeze in this place. Besides, I will soon have nothing left to eat."

The elves – for that is what they were – danced all night in the moonlight while Marie watched. But in the morning, they mounted their gossamer steeds, sat Marie between them, and flew off with her into the sky. They flew all day long above the tree-tops. "We are flying to the lake," said the elves. "There the swallows spend the night in the reeds, and they will take us with them to the warm South."

Towards evening, they could see the water glistening through the trees. Many thousand threads of gossamer came flying up, each thickly covered with elves who dismounted and gathered in a mighty oak-tree which stood on the shore of the lake among moss-covered rocks. But the gossamer steeds were allowed to fly on into the wide world. When the sun went down, the swallows arrived in a great rushing black cloud, and landed in the rushes, twittering noisily. Many of the elves flew down to greet them and nestle in their warm feathers, for the night was cold and windy. But Marie stayed up in the tree with the others. The elves had helped her to find a deserted birds' nest, and there she slept soundly, for she was very tired. But a great storm arose during the night, with wind and rain, and the wet, cold elves flew down into the rushes to be with the swallows, and forgot all about little Marie. Very early in the morning they all flew away across the sea to the warm lands of the South.

Little Marie awoke to the cawing of a raven who sat up above her in the tree singing his hungry morning song, and she rubbed her eyes in astonishment. Climbing with difficulty out of the nest on to a branch, she looked about her. There she was, high up in the old oak-tree, and all around her was loneliness and silence except for the raven sitting on his branch and cawing in a most melancholy and moving manner, for he had had no breakfast as yet, and was very hungry. Then he caught sight of Marie – and fell silent. He put his head on one side and looked thoughtfully at her with his right eye; then he tilted it the other way and looked greedily at her with his left eye, for it occurred to him that the tiny creature would make a delicious early-morning snack. Suddenly he flew off his perch and made straight for little Marie with his beak open, so that she nearly fell off the tree. Instead, she slipped hastily into a hollow branch where the angry raven could not reach her, for the opening was too narrow for his beak. So he flew away across the lake, hungry and frustrated, and the trembling little Marie could hear his hoarse cawing for a long time afterwards.

When she had recovered from her fright, she noticed that there was a light shining at the other end of the hollow branch. The oak-tree was altogether hollow, and when Marie climbed carefully along the branch, she came to the main trunk down which she peered dizzyingly. It seemed to her like a dark, bottomless abyss, and above her the sky showed through the hole at the top of the tree. Not daring to move, she sat there sadly all day long. She still had one bilberry left in her pocket which she ate, and afterwards, as evening came, she fell asleep. It was dark when she woke up again and she was very frightened, for above her in the tree sat a huge owl which screamed: "Towit, towoo!" But it soon flew away on faintly swishing wings to search for unwary mice. Then little Marie heard voices down below her in the oak, and saw a light flickering. She peeped over the edge and saw little men dressed in grey and brown moving sacks about far below her. Others were standing round them holding burning torches.

"Those must be the little dwarfs," she thought: "they are good people, and are sure to help me." So she called down the hole: "Dwarfs, dwarfs, please help me! I am sitting up here in the hollow branch!"

The little men looked up in astonishment. One of them said: "Who are you?"

"I am little Marie. The elves were going to take me with them to the warm lands of the South, but they forgot me, and left me sitting all alone up here."

"Yes," said the dwarf, "that sounds just like the elves. They are nothing but wind-bags, and one cannot rely on them. Just wait there and we'll be with you in a moment."

Soon the dwarfs brought little ladders with sharp hooks on them: with these they climbed higher and higher inside the tree, hooking one ladder on to the next, until at last they reached little Marie. The strongest dwarf took her in his arms and carried her carefully down. "You are no dwarf," he said as they reached the ground, "you are a human child. I can feel it by the warm life that flows in your veins. But how did you become so tiny?"

Marie had to tell her story over again, while the dwarfs sat chin in hand on their sacks and listened attentively.

"Poor little Marie," said the one who had carried her: "we will keep you here in our warm cave so that you do not freeze during the winter."

A carriage drawn by six mice now drew up beneath a gnarled root. The dwarfs loaded their sacks on to it, lifted little Marie on top of them, and walked beside the carriage, which slowly entered a narrow opening in the rock from which a passageway led downwards and inwards. In the light of the torches, Marie could see that the walls were studded with precious stones, veins of gold traversed the rock-face, and clear water trickled down the walls from above. At last they reached a warm, dry and brightly lit cave. The dwarfs unloaded the sacks and emptied the nuts and beechmast which filled them into store-rooms hollowed out of the walls of the cave; this kept them busy for quite a while. At some distance above floor-level, so that they had to be reached by ladders, little niches had been cut into the rock; they were filled with straw and moss with bedcovers made of mouse-skins, and this is where the dwarfs slept. Little Marie was made to sit on a stool and watch the dwarfs unloading the nuts. "Are you going to store them for Christmas?" she asked.

"No," they replied. "We eat them in the winter, when snow covers everything, and we cannot go hunting or catch fish."

Marie stayed with the dwarfs for a long time, through spring, summer, autumn and winter. She lived happily there, played with gold and precious stones, and helped the dwarfs with their work. She climbed about the rocks with them, and sailed on the lake in their little boats when the weather was calm. In the winter, they harnessed mice to their sledges and drove about in the snow, or the dwarfs skated on the lake, pushing Marie along on the ice in a tiny sled made out of half a walnut shell.

One day in the spring – it was Marie's sixteenth birthday – the dwarfs took her to a spot on the shores of the lake where huge blocks of stone lay in the high grass. Small red flowers with a strange, heavy scent grew there. The Head Dwarf pulled up one of these and gave the root to Marie. "There – eat that!" he said.

Marie obediently put the root in her mouth and said:

"How sweet it tastes!" But she had hardly spoken before she grew dizzy and sank to the ground unconscious. When she came to, she was lying on the grass all big and grown-up, while all the little dwarfs sat on a pine-branch over her head and looked down at her.

"Oh, you little dwarfs," she said. "what shall I do now?

Now I can never come into your cave again, or sleep in my dear little bed."

The Head Dwarf answered: "It is for your own good, Marie. Be patient and wait; you will be leaving us soon, and you will be happy to do so."

The dwarfs showed her a cave which was big enough for her to live in. Marie had become very beautiful. She walked lightly about with the grace of a deer, and her long golden hair hung down to her waist. The dwarfs made her a present of a white dress in which she looked like a fairy. A white stag used to graze near her cave, and he would come when she called him, and allow her to ride on his back. The dwarfs visited her every day and talked to her so that she never felt bored or lonely.

One day, she heard hunting-horns in the forest. The young duke was out hunting with his retinue. The sound drew nearer and nearer, and suddenly the white stag burst out of a thicket and knelt down before Marie so that she could mount upon his back. Marie leapt astride him, and away they went through the forest trees. But the young duke had seen the stag, blew his horn, and galloped after it on his swift black horse. The stag carried Marie along like the wind, but the duke was steadily gaining on them. He gazed in astonishment at the slender creature in white with its flying golden hair. Throwing his spear away, he spurred his horse, for he wished to catch the stag alive. As he galloped beside it, the stag grew weaker, and the duke was able to put an arm round Marie and pull her on to his horse. Relieved of its burden, the stag rushed off into the forest. But the duke put Marie before him on the saddle and rode with her to his castle, and because she was so beautiful and so graceful, he asked her to be his wife.

When the wedding was celebrated, there was music

and jubilation, and everyone ate and drank to his heart's content. The little dwarfs had their own little table placed on top of the table at which the bride and bridegroom sat, and they drank their health out of tiny mugs, and shouted: "Hurrah!" as loudly as they could.

Erica

FAR OUT UPON the brown moorland, among a few young pine-trees which only just reached to its low roof, stood a lonely cottage. It was so covered with moss and creeper that, from a distance, it might have been taken for an isolated hillock upon the wide plain, had it not been for the blue smoke which sometimes rose from its chimney. An old man lived here, quite alone except for his daughter, Erica, and his bees; there was no other house for miles around. No traveller ever approached the remote spot; there was nothing there but sky, air and the wide, flat heath, occasional pine or birch-trees growing singly or in small plantations; in the summer the purple heather in bloom full of buzzing bees and the humming of summer insects, and in winter the white expanse of snow, upon which dark pines with their snow-laden branches stood.

Little Erica was always alone. Her mother had died a long time ago and lay buried beneath a tall, lonely pine-tree beside a big rock. Here a wild rose of extraordinary beauty grew, the only one for miles around. When it flowered in springtime, it was lovely to see how it spread, letting its long, flower-covered branches climb over the grey rock and the lonely grave. This was Erica's favourite place. She often sat there looking across the sunbaked heath through the shimmering air to the delicate blue ridge of distant hills through which the far-off river ran, and where the heath ended in green meadows and undulating fields. Often, too, she would sit and listen to her father as he sat near his beehives and told her of the countries which he had visited in his youth: of the mountains and forests, foaming waterfalls and mountain streams; of broad, mighty rivers and magnificent gardens with wonderful flowers; of great cities and busy crowds of people.

"Ah, that is beautiful!" she would say. "Shall I see it all one day too?"

"Perhaps, when you are grown-up," her father replied. Then she would go back to the grey rock, look across to the blue mountains, and long for the marvels she had just heard about.

One beautiful spring morning, when the roses were in bloom and the air was full of singing larks, she was sitting at her special place again. The sun shone on her brown hair and a light breeze from the heath played with its curls. A few early butterflies were fluttering among the young roses. Then the sound of wings was heard, and a big, brightly coloured bird landed in the pine-tree above her. Erica had never seen such a wonderful bird. His plumage shone in all the loveliest colours, and when he flew down from the pine and landed near her on a little bush, his long tail floated behind him like a sparkling ribbon of flame. He sat and looked confidingly at Erica out of intelligent eyes. She stood up to get a closer view of him, but the bird flew upwards, hovered dazzlingly before her above a little hillock, and landed for an instant, glancing back at her as he did so. How lovely he was! Perhaps he would never come again. Erica felt she must see him close to, and she continued to follow him as though she were bewitched. Once she looked back. The cottage was a long way behind her, the smoke rising from it straight upwards into the sky. She felt that she ought to turn back, and the larks high in the blue sky sang:

> "Turn back, while time is on your side!
> The world is big, the world is wide.
> Turn back, while time is on your side!"

She thought she heard her father call: "Erica, Erica!" and a bee buzzed in her ear:

> "Hum – hum – don't go on!
> Hum – hum – don't go on!"

But then she looked towards the bird again as he sat a little way ahead of her on a low birch-branch and spread his wings in the sunshine so that they shone like pure gold and precious stones; and she began to follow him again.

Soon she no longer thought of turning back, but all she saw was the lovely bird with the golden tail flying ahead of her, and all she could do was to follow him. The sun burned her cheeks, but she did not feel it. Midday passed, and the sun rolled slowly downwards towards the horizon; but Erica had eyes only for the colourful bird, and followed him. By degrees the landscape grew greener and greener, the heath disappeared; flowering meadows lay before her and gently wooded hills stretched as far as the eye could see, and at last, in the late afternoon, when the sun appeared as a shining, rayless disc hanging low in the light-grey sky, Erica came to a wide river which flowed gently between its green banks. Beside the water lay a boat; the bird flew towards it and landed on the prow, looking back. Erica stepped into it, and the boat detached itself slowly from the river-bank and began to float gently downstream. Now the bird flew trustingly up to her and nestled against her hand when she gently stroked him. He shone so brightly that she thought that her fingers must kindle sparks that would fly away as she touched him.

Now the sun lay between the hills like a great round ball or a huge golden fruit in a dark shell, and so it slowly sank and went down. The afterglow remained, light mists rose above the water and the first stars began to twinkle in the blue-green sky. Erica had not noticed all this, for she had been thinking only of the lovely bird, but now she glanced up fearfully, for she realised that she was floating all alone upon the dark water. Suddenly she remembered her father whom she had deserted, and the long distance she had travelled, and knew not what to do in her distress. She looked fearfully out over the water to the banks which she could scarcely make out in the darkness and the floating mists. Meanwhile the moon had appeared large and red between the trees and, rising up into the blue, it sailed over the hills, always keeping close to her and looking earnestly down upon her. It was so horribly lonely and quiet on the river; only the little waves splashed against the boat, and sometimes a strange rushing and gurgling sound came out of the water, as though something or someone were rising from out of its depths. Then the mists grew thicker and formed themselves into all kinds of terrifying white shapes which flowed in and out of one another above the water, stretching out their arms to little Erica until she crouched down in the boat, covered her face with her hands, and started to cry with fear.

When she dared to look up again, she found herself gazing directly at the bird, who sat on the prow of the boat and had a bright, gentle aura of light all around him. She saw no more shapes in the mist, but there was darkness all around, and the boat floated in a circle of soft light. Then she felt quite comforted; she looked at the bird sitting quietly there, and gradually the gently rocking boat and the soft ripple of the waves sent her to sleep.

Next morning when she awoke, they were floating quite close to the river-bank. Huge trees bent low over the river, which washed their gnarled roots. The morning sunlight danced through the twigs upon the water, and finches warbled tirelessly in their branches. Then Erica saw slim does and huge stags wandering between the tree-trunks: squirrels climbed among the tree-tops and looked down at her. The river grew wider and wider, the banks ever further apart, and the boat floated out on to an enormous lake lying with its calm, unruffled surface reflecting the bright sunlight. Soon the shores of the lake vanished altogether, but a blue streak which looked like a distant island appeared upon the horizon. The boat gained speed and the bird, who had sat motionless until then, became restless, and kept rising into the air as though he wanted to look around, so that Erica was afraid that he might fly away: but he kept coming back and allowing her to stroke him. The opposite shore grew greener and more clearly defined; Erica could make out wooded hills and groups of trees. Then the blue and red, yellow and white of giant flowers could be seen growing on every tree and covering them completely.

Round the shore, huge reed-like plants grew thickly in the water with broad, sword-shaped leaves; from these, also, enormous flowers on long stems had sprung up, swaying and shining like white suns. Erica could not imagine how she would get through this green wall, but the boat made straight for it; then the curtain of reeds parted and the boat shot through the opening as through a green doorway, gliding smoothly on to the shore. Erica stepped out on to a beautiful, slightly sloping meadow, which was surrounded by huge trees; a gentle stream flowed through them from the top of a hill. The bird flew on ahead of Erica down a narrow path that wound its way through swaying flowers. Here and there, gigantic plants shot up between the ordinary vegetation; these had wide leaves and wonderful, shining, sunlike flowers, and giant butterflies flew about among them.

At last she stepped out of the wood on to a wide, open space covered in short grass. In its centre stood the biggest tree of all, totally surrounded by fluttering butterflies; its branches hung down to the ground as though the weight of the fabulous brightly-coloured bell-shaped flowers was too much for them to bear. Now the bird flew upwards, and disappeared among the branches of this tree.

Erica stood alone on the green grass in front of the tree, and was almost afraid, for great, grave-looking birds with long red legs and solemn beaks which looked as though they had a lot to say were walking about there; but they did not bother her, only looked at her in a friendly way. All of a sudden, the branches of the tree parted, and a beautiful woman in a long white dress stepped out, who took Erica's hand, and said: "Dear Erica, will you stay with me on my lovely island?"

Then Erica suddenly remembered her old father and the little cottage on the heath, and the rose-tree on her mother's grave, and she cried out: "No, no! I must go! My father is grieving for me! Oh – I have been very wicked to have run away like this!" And she began to cry.

"Be still, Erica," said the lovely woman, and stroked her brown hair. "You shall see him again soon; but it is a long way from here, and you must rest."

So saying, she took Erica under the flowering tree whose huge, wide-spreading branches formed a wonderful sort of cave. The light breeze hummed through the twigs and created a soft whispering and ringing like gentle music. Here they sat down upon rich coverlets, which were spread upon the ground, before a festive meal served in delicately wrought dishes of gold and silver, and there was sparkling red wine in crystal bottles, followed by golden fruit shining in bowls made of precious stones. The fairy took a goblet of red wine and gave it to Erica to drink. At that moment, she seemed once more to hear the lark singing:

"Turn back, while time is on your side!
Turn back, turn back – : the world is wide!"

and like a cry from very far away came the faint voice of her father: "Erica! Erica!"

But the fairy smiled sweetly and said: "Drink the wine, Erica." And it had such an intoxicating perfume that she could not help lifting the goblet to her lips and taking a deep draught. At this, a rose-pink light appeared before her eyes, there was a rushing sound in her ears as though everything she had known up to that moment was being carried away from her. Then she heard a melodious ringing as of bells tolling, and when she came to her senses, she had forgotten everything: her father, the lonely cottage on the heath – and all the rest. If she attempted to think back into the past, all was darkness, and only the present was beautiful, rose-pink and happy. The fairy drew her to her and kissed her, for now she belonged only to her, and then they ate some of the lovely fruit, until the grave birds came and carried away the dishes in their beaks, a service they performed silently and efficiently. Then a carriage drawn by two white peacocks flew up, and the fairy said: "Dear Erica, I am going away now, and will not be back till tomorrow evening; in the meantime, you may like to explore the island. One of the birds will be your guide and you may ride on his back if you want to: there is no need to be afraid."

They stepped out of the tree-cave, and the fairy flew away in her carriage – high up into the blue air – until

before she vanished into the sky her dazzling white gown made her look like a shining star in the distance.

Erica walked about and examined the tree, which stood before her like a mighty, colourful mountain covered in bell-shaped flowers. She saw that new flowers continuously grew and swiftly faded and died, but they never fell to the ground, for as they fell, they turned into butterflies, and fluttered away into the wood. There were fruits, too, which sat upon the tree like shining globes. From time to time, one of these burst open, and out flew a glittering bird which sat in the branches, or flew off into the wood. While she continued to stand and stare, a huge bird approached, bowed gravely before her, and then walked away in front of her, signing to her to follow him. When he had led her around for a while, and she saw how gentle and tame he was, Erica felt that she would like to climb on to his back, which she managed quite easily from the branch of a tree. But what a fright she got when he suddenly started to run, spread his enormous wings, and rose with her into the air. She clutched his feathers in terror; but soon she was no longer afraid, for she felt as safe sitting upon his back as though she were in a cradle, and it was wonderful to look down from such a height upon land and water. At first the bird rose high in the sky, so that the island in the lake looked like a coloured carpet on a blue background. But then he floated in slow circles in the air, and sank gently down towards the island. Meanwhile, evening had come, and the red sun was sinking from the cloudless sky into the lake; and the bird, descending swiftly earthwards, deposited Erica in the grass near the flowering tree.

Now fireflies flew about in the twilight like tiny lanterns and one of these sat in every flower and illuminated it, so that all the flowers gave out a soft white or coloured light. But two great lantern-butterflies flew before Erica all the time, and lit the way for her. As she followed with her eyes the shining beetles which passed one another in the darkness like shooting stars, she suddenly noticed a bright light high up in the dark sky, and the nearer it got, the larger it seemed to grow. Soon she recognised the fairy in her glittering carriage drawn by the white peacocks, each of whom now wore a radiant star upon his head. The fairy greeted Erica, and took her under the tree, where the birds had already suspended a soft, swaying hammock beneath the branches. Here Erica lay down to sleep. The bellflowers shone softly down upon her through the branches; now and then a wandering beetle buzzed through the tree like an erring spark; but the two lantern-butterflies had extinguished their light and sat at her head, fanning her with their wings, and what with the humming of the beetles and the gentle cradle-song of the tree, she fell sweetly and soundly asleep.

So Erica lived for many days upon the beautiful island with the fairy. In the morning, when the rim of the sun was just showing above the lake and its first rays touched the tops of the trees, she would jump out of her swaying bed and climb into the trees by means of one of the low-hanging branches, which formed a natural stairway. Here the fairy slept in a cave densely woven of leaves and twigs. Then they would climb together to the top of the tree, from which one could look out over the entire island. Here they sat upon thickly interwoven branches and Erica combed the long golden hair of the fairy with a silver comb. They were surrounded by dancing butterflies, and the birds flew above their heads. The verdant woods lay all around, and beyond them stretched the blue lake – on and on until it met the horizon like a fine line in the misty distance. Soon afterwards, the fairy would fly away in her peacock carriage, and Erica spent the whole day alone. She played with flowers, butterflies and birds, and for a long time she was completely happy and contented.

But then, the island suddenly did not seem beautiful to her any more. Nothing changed: everything was always the same. The great tree blossomed and blossomed, the flowers fell off and turned into butterflies, and the shining birds kept on flying out of the bursting fruit. The sky was eternally clear, bright and blue, and the fairy flew away every morning and came back every evening: and so it went on each and every day. Now one morning, as Erica sat in bed looking cross because she was thinking of the long day that lay ahead and of the everlasting colourful, silent birds and butterflies, and all the now so familiar splendour, she thought she heard a bird singing softly from far away. It sounded so melancholy and so nostalgic that a wonderful sensation gripped her heart; as she listened to the song, she kept feeling that she ought to remember something that had once happened to her, but it would not come back to her. She got up, and followed the sound, but it grew ever more distant, and at last it could be heard no more. Now she suddenly realised that she had never yet heard a bird sing on the island, for the coloured birds were dumb, and their voices were never heard in any part of the island.

So she ran quickly to the fairy, and cried: "Tell me why the birds don't sing here?"

The fairy smiled and said: "They will soon start to sing if you touch them with this little stick." And she handed her a small golden wand.

So Erica ran happily off into the wood, enticed the birds to her and touched them with the wand, and they immediately began a lovely, fluting song which echoed through the whole wood. Erica rejoiced, and touched the big birds on the grass plot as well; but they bowed deeply to her and emitted such a hoarse, raucous bellow that she took fright and ran into the wood to escape the noise.

On this day, a complete change took place on the island. Where there had been utter silence, there was now a warbling, exulting and fluting enough to deafen one, and Erica ran about tirelessly touching the birds with her wand, so that every one of them should sing. Towards evening, however, one after the other fell silent, and eventually the island was as quiet as before.

The next morning, when the sun rose, Erica was already awake, but the quiet was still unbroken; the birds flew about, their plumage bright in the sunlight, but none of them sang a note. The fairy explained: "The touch of the wand only works for a day. In the evening, the birds stop singing, and they only regain their voice if the wand touches them anew."

That day Erica only touched a few birds with her wand and listened to their lovely song; and it was not long before this song began to pall. The birds sat there in the sunshine, let their fine plumage glisten, and sang their song over and over again, always as lovely, always the same, as though their insides were made of clockwork. It seemed to Erica that the main point of the song was missing, but she could not say what it was. In the end, she knew it by heart: "Tireli – tirela, gluck – gluck – gluck – zizizizi!" Then she ran away so as not to hear it any more, and in the evening she was glad that the birds were quiet at last.

That night, she couldn't go to sleep. She was sad without knowing why, and stared into the dark branches of the tree through which the flowers' gentle light shone upon her. Then, once again, she heard the soft song of the same bird, and it seemed much closer now, as though the bird were hovering in the air above the tree. Once again she pondered and thought and thought, but she could not remember. She was overcome with a deep longing; it seemed as though the bird's melancholy song were drawing her away, as though she must fly after it at any moment. At last the song grew more distant, and as it faded, so she fell asleep.

After this, Erica lost all desire to hear the birds sing; she moped about, and nothing gave her any pleasure. The new bird sang every evening now, and sounded as though he were sitting in the big tree itself, and she could scarcely sleep at night for the nostalgia and restlessness the song aroused in her; but she did not know what it was she longed for.

One morning, the fairy said to her: "You aren't as happy as you used to be, dear Erica. I expect you need some company. Just take your little golden wand and touch the flowers with it; then they will turn into lovely children and you will be able to play with them."

Erica was full of joy, ran into the wood, and touched her favourite white flower. Immediately the flower opened, and out popped a bright, childish face with soft flaxen curls: the white petals flowed downwards to form a dress, and there stood the dearest little girl smiling at her. They kissed one another, and then Erica touched even more flowers. The red ones became black-haired children with shining black eyes, the blue ones were fair, and the yellow ones had brown hair.

During that whole day, life was marvellous. The children tumbled about in the big tree on whose broad, moss-covered branches they could run about as though they were steps, and among whose thickly-leaved twigs they sat as though on soft cushions. And they played: "Hide and Seek" and "Visiting" and "How do you like your Neighbour?" and then they all danced on the grass until evening came.

When the sun was about to go down, the children disappeared one after another into the wood; only the first one remained, the one that had come from the white flower. Erica wanted to keep her with her to sleep with her in her hammock because she loved her so much, but the little girl eluded her grasp and ran off into the twilit wood. But despite this, Erica was still quite happy, for she thought: "She will come back tomorrow, and then we will have even lovelier games than today." And with this thought, she fell asleep.

But the next morning no children were to be seen, although Erica looked everywhere for them, and called out to them in the wood. She was forced to resort to her wand and transform more flowers. But now she was not so happy as she had been the day before, because she kept wondering what had happened to all the other children.

On this day, they all rode up into the sky on the backs of the big birds, and Erica almost forgot her anxiety as she played in the air with the colourful band of children, while the birds wheeled about, flew over one another, and then sank gently earthwards with great circular movements. Then they played by the stream as it flowed gently by, built boats out of big leaves, harnessed dragonflies to them, and sailed them right to the shores of the lake. There they sat in the rushes and blew on little pipes they had cut out of the reeds, and played with the fish which stuck their heads confidingly up out of the water. But, as evening approached, they danced once more on the grass under the tree. When the sun began to go down, the children started to run off into the wood again, and before Erica had time to look around, only one was left, the one she had just been playing with.

Then Erica put her arms around her, and cried: "You

shall not run away! You must tell me where you go to: I want to know!" But the child twisted and turned, trying to get away. Just as she had managed to extricate herself from Erica's grasp, the last glint of sunlight vanished over the horizon; at this moment, the child shrivelled up, and a withered white flower lay at Erica's feet. She cried out loud, and knelt down and kissed the flower and touched it with her wand, but it remained faded and dead.

As she lay weeping miserably in her swaying bed, she heard the soft, delicate song again, and it came nearer and nearer, as though the bird were hopping down towards her from twig to twig. Then she heard a light fluttering sound, and now she could clearly see, lit by the brightness which radiated from the flowers, a little grey bird sitting on a twig just above her head. It sang and sang so beautifully that Erica's eyes filled with tears.

"Don't sing so loudly, little bird: the fairy might hear you!" said Erica. And now she could understand everything the bird was singing to her.

"She cannot hear me, she cannot hear me. Only you can hear me: it is for you that I sing. Can you still remember, Erica? Do you know the little grey cottage on the heath, where the humming-beehives stand? Have you ever thought of the old man, your father, who loves you so much, and who is all alone now, all alone? Do you remember the rose-tree on your mother's grave under the tall, lonely pine? Erica! Erica!"

And the memories returned to Erica as though out of a fog. She saw everything that the bird sang about, and was overcome by violent homesickness. "I must get away, I must get away, I must go home," she said.

But the little bird went on singing: "How lovely the heath is, how lovely! When the larks hover above it like singing stars. Or when it is in purple flower all the way to the blue horizon, and the bees buzz in the perfumed heather, and the sun sails high in the blue sky and shines burningly down, so that the air trembles above the flowering sea, and blue butterflies flutter above it. How lovely the heath is, how lovely!''

While he sang, the bird had flown off, and the song grew fainter and fainter, and as if from high in the sky Erica heard: ''How lovely the heath is, how lovely!'' once more. Then there was silence.

Erica sat up in bed. ''I must go, I must go, I must go back home!'' she said. But how could she get away? There was water all around, and the fairy would certainly not let her go; she was afraid to ask her, but she must get away, or else she would die of homesickness! Then she thought of her father again, and of his sorrow at her desertion of him, and she cried herself to sleep.

The next morning, she ran around the whole island along the shore beside the water, looking for a gap in the impenetrable wall of reeds. But they stood all round, close together, their sharp sword-shaped leaves like shields, and cut her hands until they bled whenever she tried to get through them. At last she remembered the stream; she hurried to it and was delighted to see that it flowed into the lake through an opening in the reed-wall. Quickly she sat down and made herself a boat out of a huge, tough leaf, and beside her on a twig sat the little grey bird and sang while she worked. She made great haste, for she had to get away before the fairy returned. The sun was sinking towards the horizon as the boat was finished. Then she broke off a branch to serve as an oar, climbed cheerfully into the fragile craft, and pushed it out into the water; the bird flew on to her shoulder.

At first she rowed between the wall of reeds, for the reed-beds stretched far out into the lake. Just as she rounded a bend and was about to sail out into the open, she saw two big birds standing in the water on either side of the gap, like two sentinels keeping watch. They opened their huge beaks, clattered them threateningly, and pecked at Erica.

"The wand, the wand!" sang the bird in her ear. When she touched the birds with it, they bowed so low to her that their long beaks dipped into the water, and let her sail by. So she rowed out on to the lake that lay quiet and calm in the evening sun, and on and on until the island lay far behind her. The sun went down in heavy cloud which lay all along the horizon, and the sunset cast its red glow over the lake. Then the light died and the water darkened and there was darkness all around; only the myriad stars sparkled in the sky, and their flickering reflections rested in the depths of the lake. Soon the moon emerged from the clouds and made a shining pathway upon the surface of the water, and Erica followed it on and on, and rowed until her hands were blistered. "Bear up, bear up!" sang the little bird.

When the fairy came home and could not find Erica anywhere, she rode one of the birds into the sky and saw her rowing up the path of moonlight far out into the lake. But outside the island, she had no power to get her back. However, as she was very angry, she stirred up a terrible storm on the lake so as to drown Erica. Clouds covered the face of the moon so that it became completely dark, and the wind rose howling over the water so that the waves reared up and bore down upon Erica like dark monsters with white crests, threatening to engulf her. She sat in the little boat and stared anxiously out into the night. But the bird sang in her ear: "Bear up, bear up!" So she took fresh courage, and baled out the water that kept pouring into the boat with her small hands. But the storm became wilder, and the waves threw the boat about as though it were a rubber ball; then the biggest wave of all towered up and broke over her, and she lost consciousness.

When she came to, she was lying on the green grass on the shore of the lake, which was still a little disturbed. The sun shone through the trees, and sparkled on the water. A great, wild wood lay ahead of her, many miles in circumference. She walked through it all day, while the bird flew ahead and showed her the way. When she grew tired, he sang, and her longing drove her on over mountains and through valleys. The thorns tore her skin and the sharp stones cut her feet; but she heeded neither pain nor hunger; all she ate was a few berries picked from the bushes as she passed. At night, as she lay down on the moss to try to sleep, wild beasts roared all around her, and enormous owls with glowing eyes flew noiselessly over her head and called eerily: "Shuhoo, shuhoo!" But the bird sang in her ear, and she listened only to him.

She had been wandering thus for many days when, one morning, the wood began to thin out until soon there were only a few isolated pine-trees scattered here and there; and then she stepped out upon the wide heath, that stretched away as far as the eye could see. Erica's heart rejoiced: she threw herself on the ground and kissed the earth. There was still a long way to go; the sun burned down from the sky; there was no water for miles around, so that her thirst became well-nigh unbearable. But the little bird flew before her and sang, and she no longer felt the torturing thirst. At last, in the afternoon, she saw blue smoke on the horizon, that rose up into the still air, and her steps quickened. Then the grey cottage appeared between the young pines: it lay in the distance like a small hillock in a bluish haze. And in the evening, when the sun was just about to go down behind it, she reached it in breathless haste, and cried out: "Father, father!" He was standing beside his beehives and turned quickly, and she flew into his arms, crying and sobbing for joy.

But the grey bird rose carolling into the sky to join the

larks in singing the praises of the quiet, shining evening, and the sun sank like a great red-gold disc behind the horizon. The afterglow filled the sky, and the father pressed his Erica to his heart, stroked her brown hair, and kissed her. And all was well again.

The Wizard

1 Mr Sugarman

ANGLEBURG was a strange and twisted old town. The main streets were narrow and crooked enough, but the side-alleys were even narrower and more crooked, besides which, they ran into one another in the oddest way, or ended unexpectedly in a canal full of murky-looking water, or emerged into dark courtyards or blind alleys; so that Angleburg really was a vexing town for strangers to visit, for it took so long before anyone could learn to find his way about in its odd intricacies. There were curious dark archways, which echoed resoundingly whenever a cart passed through them, and nowhere else in the world could there possibly have been found such a collection of quaint old gabled houses. Some were bending forwards, as though they had lost something in the street and were looking down to see if they could find it; some were leaning back with an air of refinement, as though the world and its doings were no concern of theirs; yet others had subsided a little in the direction of the house next door, and seemed relieved that, by leaning up against it, they had been prevented from falling over altogether. In a few alley-ways, the upper storeys of the houses overhung the lower ones, so that the taller the houses were, the closer together they grew, until eventually only a narrow strip of sky showed between them. If two good friends happened to live opposite one another, they could shake hands to say good morning, and one could light his pipe at the other's spillikin. What a profusion of unusual dormer-windows, quaint narrow casements and complicated wood-carvings; what a countless array of curious towers, gables and creaking weather-vanes: what a quantity of twisted inn-signs and painted trade-boards there were in this town! Anyone walking through these quiet streets on a moonlit night, and seeing all the strangely contorted gables and crenallations silhouetted against the sky, while the bright moonlight fell upon the grotesquely grimacing beam-heads, and an ancient house stared out of the darkness like a grey face with open jaws, could not be blamed for thinking that the whole scene had been conjured up by magic, and would vanish like a dream at the first hint of sunlight.

Now there lived quite alone in one of the oddest-looking houses near the town-hall an old man whose name was Sugarman. Strange rumours were abroad concerning this man. He was generally supposed to be a wizard, and people said that he could work better magic than anyone else in the whole country. It was said that, long years before, a strange man had entered the town in a gilded coach; he was supposed to have been a Count. He took the best rooms in the "Golden Lion". He had come especially to see Mr Sugarman, so as to learn sorcery from him. In return for a great bag of gold – some say that it was a sack containing a bushel of Spanish doubloons; others maintain that it was merely a money-belt full of coins such as the cattle-dealers wear – anyway, the story goes that the old man was prepared to teach his arts to the stranger in return for a lot of money. So, day after day, these two shut themselves away in the old house, and anyone who happened to be passing by heard many strange sounds, and among them a sort of nasal singing. From time to time, a purple plume of smoke rose from the chimney, and at these moments the whole neighbourhood smelled of hyacinths and narcissi, even though it was the middle of winter. One evening, the whole house was illuminated from within by a red light, so that everyone thought it was on fire. But the people who ran to see the blaze saw, instead, through the windows, Mr Sugarman and the stranger sitting in the midst of the dark-red glow, like two fiery beings drinking flaming punch, whereat they were more than a little horrified.

Finally, Mr Sugarman said that he could teach nothing more to the stranger. But the latter frowned threateningly when he asked Mr Sugarman whether he had really taught him everything he knew. Yes – indeed he had – said Mr Sugarman. All of a sudden, the stranger drew forth a double-barrelled pistol and fired both barrels at the wizard, because he desired to do away with him so that *he* might be the greatest wizard in all the land. But Mr Sugarman only smiled a little, and when the powder-smoke had cleared, he was seen to be holding a bullet between the thumb and forefinger of each hand. Then, making a graceful bow, he said: "I kept that trick up my sleeve, Count!"

The Count rushed off to the "Golden Lion" in a great rage, ordered his carriage, and drove away. Some people who are generally reliable swear that he left the town by all four gates at the same time. But they also say that Mr Sugarman, too, was to be seen at all four gates simultaneously, bowing mockingly to the carriage as it passed him.

Many such stories were passed around, and the wizard was so feared by all and sundry that even the cheekiest street-urchin did not dare to mock him, although this cannot have been easy considering the strange attire he appeared in in public. One boy, who stuck out his tongue and thumbed his nose at the old man, wished that he had not; for during that entire day, he could not get his tongue back into his mouth or his thumb away from his nose. Only when the sun went down was the spell broken. But this universal fear did not prevent many people from knocking at his door at twilight with various special requests; for Mr Sugarman was very clever at concocting many magical and secret remedies, and for a good sum of money, he sold strangely shaped phials containing love-potions and other liquids which had a narcotic aroma; they were effective against all kinds of illness and other troubles. He knew how to prepare a fumigating powder whose odour was pleasant to the human nose, but was unbearable to any form of vermin. Only a small pinch of this powder was needed to fumigate an entire house, with the result that whining and squeaking emanated from every corner, and rats and mice, bedbugs and cockroaches and any other pests that happened to be infesting it, rushed out of the place as fast as they could, and were not seen again for many years afterwards. Furthermore, it was a very strange fact that Mr Sugarman never went out shopping in the market, nor did he go to the baker, butcher or wine-merchant, and yet he lacked nothing – indeed, he partook of the most delectable food. An old woman who had called to get a concoction for her sick cow, had peeked through the kitchen door, and seen a hare which was turning itself over the fire on a spit, while delicious fritters bubbled in a frying-pan. But on the kitchen table sat the wizard's monkey. He wore a clean apron, and was in the act of plucking two plump snipe. The cowherd, who grazed his cattle near the town wall which bordered Mr Sugarman's garden, also had a curious tale to tell. Once he had seen a hare burst out of the wood at full speed and, although hares cannot normally climb like cats, this one had scaled the steep wall, and jumped down into the wizard's garden.

2 *Wendelin*

In the same town, Angleburg, in one of the narrow, gabled houses, there lived a widow with her only son, Wendelin. Although she was a poor woman, who earned a scanty living by spinning and taking in washing, she managed to put by enough to see that little Wendelin was always cleanly and neatly dressed, and to send him to a good school. But when the boy was fifteen years old, his mother fell ill and died. The funeral expenses took what little money was left, and Wendelin found himself alone and penniless in the world. True, a weaver for whom his mother had often spun yarn had offered to take him on as an apprentice; but Wendelin could not bear the idea of work which had to be carried on in dark rooms full of pale-faced people; he would rather have been a gardener whose job takes him out in the fresh air among trees and flowers. But hunger is painful, and probably he would have become a weaver in the end if something had not unexpectedly intervened.

One day, when the last provisions in his mother's frugal store-cupboard had been eaten, and he was plagued by hunger, he walked the streets full of gloomy thoughts, and because he had tired himself out and was deep in melancholy reflections upon his sad situation, he did not notice where he was. He sat down on a stone right in front of the wizard's house, at a spot which was given a wide berth by the fearful inhabitants of Angleburg, and the realisation of his poverty and solitude so overcame him, that he covered his face with his hands and began to sob bitterly. It was just about noon, and the streets were empty and sunny. Smoke rose vertically from all the surrounding chimney-pots into the quiet sky, and bore witness to the boiling and roasting that was going on, but alas, no hearth was preparing anything for poor, lonely Wendelin.

As he sat there, while the tears ran through his fingers and dropped on to the hot paving-stones, he heard the rattle of a window opening behind him, and at the same moment, a delicious aroma of roasting and baking filled the air, and a thin, hoarse voice spoke: "Are you hungry, my boy? Come in: the birdies are roasting in the pan and are waiting for you. Can you hear them chirping?"

Wendelin jumped up, and saw Mr Sugarman standing at the open window with an artful grin on his face. Thin black hair hung down on either side of that small, sinister, bird-like face, and on his head he wore a red velvet skull-cap. Otherwise his dress consisted of a long and ancient coat, which he wore all the year round. It had a fur collar, and had once been green, but now it was so faded and dirty that no artist could have said what colour it was. But Wendelin could see past Mr Sugarman's shoulder into the kitchen in the background, from which the lovely, penetrating odours proceeded. The sunlight shone in diagonal stripes through the bluish vapour, and an appetising bubbling and frying sound could be heard.

Despite his hunger, Wendelin did not dare to accept the invitation, for he shared the whole town's fear of the wizard. But, because he had no idea what to say, he stood there completely dumbfounded, and was just about to run away when the old man spoke again: "Little coward, what are you afraid of? I like your face, and wish you nothing but good. Come inside, you fool, and listen to what I have to say to you; afterwards you can still do whatever you have a mind to. Or would you rather go hungry, and allow yourself to be shut up in a gloomy room at a boring loom? You will be much better off in beautiful gardens among trees and flowers."

The old man talked on about this and that, and it was

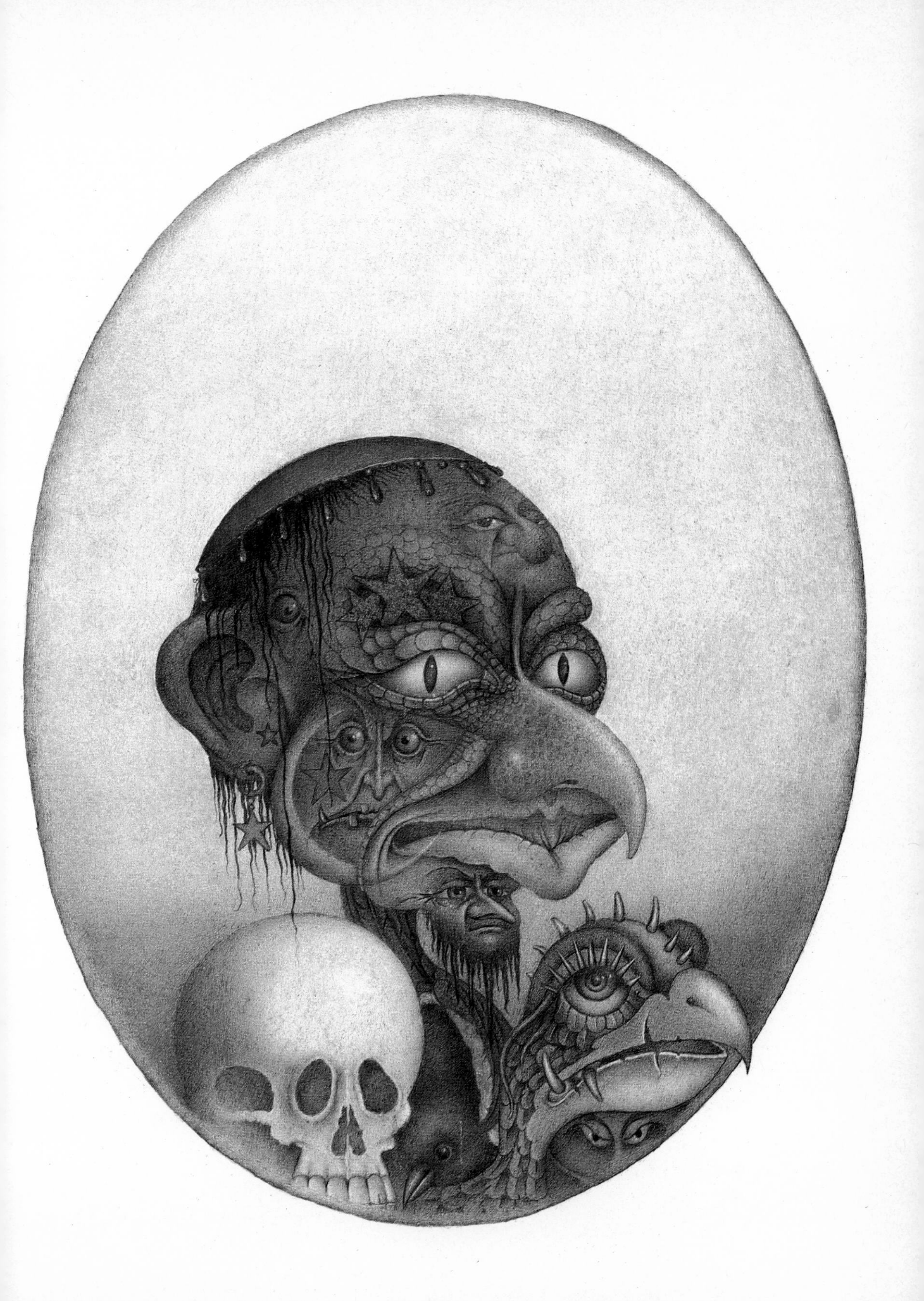

strange how his face appeared to Wendelin to grow more handsome, until it seemed to him that he had never seen a more friendly or pleasantly-spoken gentleman; and before he really knew what he was doing, the boy had the doorknob in his hand, and was walking through the front door. As he opened it, a carillon of bells rang out, and, as though this were not enough, the house reverberated with chiming and striking and cries of: "Cuckoo!" and "Cock-a-doodle-do!" so that the din was terrific. A small, odd-looking little white dog belonging to that parsimonious breed that tends to make use of only three of its four legs, ran up to Wendelin and yapped like anything in a fine, hoarse voice. It sounded so ugly and vicious, though, that it was quite obvious that, if it had been bigger and stronger, it would have leapt at his throat and pulled him to the ground. Suddenly Mr Sugarman was standing next to the boy, who had not heard him coming, because he wore felt slippers. "Come on, come on!" he said, took Wendelin by the hand, and led him into a big room which looked out on to the garden. This was probably the wizard's study, because the walls were lined with rows of leather-bound books whose backs were decorated with strange, coloured figures. On the top of the book-shelves there were some hideous stuffed animals, and skeletons, and glass jars in which snakes, big lizards and other ugly creatures were preserved in spirits. An enormous green-glazed porcelain stove stood against the wall, and horrid grimacing faces and witches' heads stared out from its tiles, and other nasty things besides.

In the middle of the room a table stood with three chairs round it; one of these was unusually high, like a baby-chair, and built to look like a small tower. Suddenly the door opened and the monkey came running in on three legs; with the fourth, he was carrying a plate. He jumped on to the table, put the plate down, grinned and gnashed his teeth at Wendelin, and ran out again. He kept running backwards and forwards very quickly, bringing one thing at a time, until the table was laid. Then, walking on his hind legs with care, and frowning anxiously, he carried in the soup. The little dog was lifted up on to the third chair, and sat at the table, delicately lapping up the soup from his plate, and stopping occasionally to yap angrily at Wendelin.

But Wendelin had never before tasted such delicious soup. It flowed beneficently into his hungry stomach, and as it did so, the blood began to course warmly through his veins, so that he thought he had never in his life felt so well. Later on, there were small roast birds with apple sauce accompanied by a clear, golden wine which had the aroma of the pure breath of spring, and was so well-chilled that the glasses were beaded with pearly droplets. Lastly, some little pancakes were served, filled with raspberry jam, and followed by crystallised fruits. Wendelin, for whom potatoes in their jackets with herrings was already a banquet, thought that the king himself could not dine more festively than this. When Mr Sugarman saw how the boy tucked in, he chuckled and said: "You can eat like that every day: you only have to wish it."

After the meal, he explained to Wendelin what he required of him. He was to work in the garden and look after the flowers and special herbs, for Mr Sugarman found it hard to bend down these days. In return, he would be paid a French dollar a month, and free board and lodging, as well as one new suit every year. As Wendelin had wanted to be a gardener, and the wizard now seemed to him to be a friendly little man and no longer terrifying, he agreed to this arrangement.

3 *Strange Goings-On*

As time passed, Wendelin found it difficult to get used to the peculiarities of the house, for quite unheard of things took place there. Even in the garden, and curiously enough especially at midday, he sometimes found himself shuddering. This small garden-space was enclosed by the house in front, the town wall behind, and two high walls on either side. The wizard grew a variety of plants and herbs which he needed for his magic arts and secret potions, for instance: Squinancy Wort, Devil's Bite, White Orantis, Witchherb, Boar-Root, Henbane, Pimpernel and so on. Some exotic plants grew and blossomed there, such as Wendelin had never seen before. Some had flowers which looked like little red hearts suspended from a thread. The juice from the root of this plant was supposed to be effective against the pains of love. Others took the form of flies or butterflies or funny little men, or tiny carriages drawn by doves. One kind of plant shot great stalks upwards from a circle of round, blue-green leaves, and these stalks were wreathed with huge trumpet-flowers that looked as though they were made of transparent wax, and the bottom of each trumpet was stained with a purple glow. Then there were plants which grew long tendrils and attached themselves to everything. Others stood up stiffly, covered in thorns and with intricately serrated leaves, and their flowers looked out of a thorny cap like angry red faces. Around noon, a stupefying, heavy odour filled the enclosed space, and at this hour, it gave Wendelin the creeps, because a strange agitation took place among the flowers. Sometimes it seemed as though faces peered out from them, and then put their heads together and giggled. Once, when he trod on a long tendril which had climbed on to a step, he clearly heard a high, pained squeak, and another time, when he pulled up a root, it sighed and moaned just like a person, so that he dropped it in alarm. But he was even more alarmed when the root immediately slipped back into its hole, and could plainly be heard laughing. Many such strange things happened to him, which was why he didn't like working in the garden at noon.

But the house was uncanny too, for a peculiar hurrying and scurrying could be heard at twilight. Wendelin didn't believe that rats and mice were solely responsible for the noises, because he had sometimes clearly seen little men with big heads, who were bustling about with brooms and scrubbing-brushes. Probably brownies or pixie-folk who looked after the house, because it was always swept and dusted, although no one lifted a hand to do any housework.

From time to time, Mr Sugarman had an odd visitor. The front door opened, all the bells rang, but there was no one to be seen. Then the shuffling noise that bedroom-slippers make could be heard in the passage, and there was a sharp, bony tap on the door. Mr Sugarman opened it, and let whatever it was come in, and was very polite, almost servile, to this thing that no one saw. If Wendelin happened to be there, he got pushed out in a hurry, and then he heard the wizard talking loudly and eagerly, and a hoarse voice replying. After a while, the spectre went away in the manner of its arrival. Usually Mr Sugarman was very pale and excited after it had left, and had to fortify himself with a good deal of wine.

Wendelin slept upstairs in an attic room, in which every kind of dried herb hung beneath the roof, and where several strange old pieces of furniture stood. The walls were hung with a very ancient woven tapestry in which the art of the weaver had portrayed many colourful, fantastic birds which perched upon garlands of flowers. Once at midnight, when the full moon shone into the room, Wendelin was awakened by a sweet singing and ringing. The moon shone brightly upon the old tapestry, and he could see that all the birds were singing merrily: he could clearly make out their moving beaks, and their crops filling with air. They did not fall silent until the clock-tower struck one.

But gradually Wendelin got used to all these extraordinary events, and after a while, he scarcely paid them any attention. As he was so well fed in return for his light work in the garden, and ate his fill of delicious game and other good things, he became bigger and stronger, and his cheeks were rosy like apples. He had discovered, too, how Mr Sugarman managed to get hold of all the game. He set his traps behind the great porcelain stove; then he opened the window and made a lot of signs in the air. Very soon, something dashed in from outside, and the next moment, there was a lot of wriggling and jiggling behind the stove. When he went to have a look, the snares contained a hare, or a brace of fat partridges, snipe, quail, fieldfare or their like; whichever animal or bird the wizard fancied was sure to hang in the snare. If, on the other hand, the supply of flour, seasoning, butter or anything else had run out in the store-cupboard, a drawer which usually contained the item was filled with sand from a pit in the yard, and the supply was immediately restored. The wizard could probably have become a rich man by selling wares so cheaply acquired, but there was an attendant snag to this, for the magic worked only for the supply of his own house. If he sold any of it, it turned straight back into sand again.

4 *The Magpie Shackerack*

In a corner between the wall and the great, green stove sat the magpie Shackerack in a wire cage. She was nearly as clever as a human being, and could speak, whistle, laugh and bark amongst other things. The little dog, whose name was Tipperling, could not stand her, and often stood in front of her cage and yapped savagely at her. The magpie paid little attention to this other than to look at him mockingly out of one eye, imitate his bark, and then laugh. This made the dog so angry that his eyes popped out of his head, and he barked himself nearly hoarse.

The magpie seemed to fancy Wendelin, and every time he came into the room, she cried in a friendly voice: "Wendelin!" and then whistled in a particularly attractive way. One day, Mr Sugarman had gone out, after the invisible being had visited him the day before, and talked to him long and vehemently. Hardly were he and Tipperling out of the door than the boy heard a voice from the house repeatedly calling: "Wendelin! Wendelin!" Wonderingly, he followed the direction of the voice, and found that it was the magpie, who was hopping restlessly about in her cage and constantly calling his name. As soon as he entered the room, she said: "Wendelin, beware!"

"Of whom should I beware?" he asked.

"They want to sell your soul," said the bird.

When Wendelin asked what this was supposed to mean, the magpie Shackerack told him strange things.

"The wizard," said she, "obtained power over me through a cunning ruse, though he does not have so much control over us magpies as over the other stupid animals which run blindly into his snares. He knows that I possess, safely hidden away, the ring of the great magician Girandola, which was stolen from him by one of my ancestors, and has been handed down from generation to generation of our family ever since. He desires above all things to get hold of this ring, because the possessor of this jewel holds sway over the spirits of earth, air, fire and water, and is thus the greatest magician in the world. Every day he pesters and torments me to make me hand over the ring to him, but up till now, I have stood my ground, for I heartily detest this wizard. He has threatened to kill me on Twelfth Night, when the time is propitious, and burn me into a powder which can cure epilepsy; but I only laugh, because he is not likely to destroy his only hope of getting his hands on the ring. I have now built all my hopes of freedom on you, more especially since I can do you a great service in return, and besides, you would be lost without my warning. Yesterday, the invisible guest was here again. Do you know who it is? It is the greatest sorcerer of all, old Urian himself. In return for his magic knowledge, Mr Sugarman sold his soul to him, and at the end of this year, the time will be up. But he can extend it by ten years if he can supply Urian with a new soul, and yours is the one he has decided upon. Without my warning, you would have been lost without recall, for you are young and inexperienced, and have no weapons against the arts of the Devil or the power of evil potions which confuse the senses. Give me back my freedom, and I will repay you by putting you in possession of the magic ring for a whole year. If you carry it with you, you need never fear any wizard, for no power in the world can harm you."

Wendelin was exceedingly shocked and surprised by the story the magpie Shackerack had told him, but he still hesitated and asked questions and wanted to know more. But the magpie cried: "Time is running out: in an hour, Mr Sugarman will be back, and I need almost that long to fetch the ring." Half stunned and totally bewildered, Wendelin opened the cage door and the window; in a moment, the magpie was free and had flown off. Soon she had disappeared behind the town-wall, and now Wendelin was overcome by deep remorse at what he had done. How could he be certain that the cunning magpie was not deceiving him, and that she would keep her promise to him? How horribly slowly the time crawled by. Every other minute he gave a start, thinking that he heard the returning steps of Mr Sugarman. One moment he ran to the front window and looked fearfully down into the quiet, sunny street below: the next he ran back to the other window and looked up into the blue summer sky. The clock ticked so slowly, and the hands scarcely seemed to move; he would have liked to have pushed them forward, if this could have helped.

Three quarters of an hour had passed in this way, and he was growing ever more fearful, because there was still no sign of the magpie. Then the sounds of shuffling steps were audible from the street below and Wendelin knew that Mr Sugarman was coming. The boy stood there deathly pale and trembling in every limb. Now the door opened downstairs and all the bells rang. Wendelin was just about to jump out of the window, run through the garden, climb the town-wall and run away into the wide world when, at the last moment, just as Mr Sugarman reached for the door-handle, the sound of wings was heard, and the magpie landed on the window-sill, letting the ring fall from her beak. Wendelin pocketed it quickly, the magpie sang out:

"Twist it once around, my dear
and the spirits will appear."

And then, just as the wizard stepped into the room, she flew away, laughing loudly. The wizard rushed towards Wendelin in a towering rage. "You have let the magpie go!" he yelled.

"Yes," said Wendelin quite calmly.

At first, Mr Sugarman was stiff with anger. His eyes protruded, his lips trembled, and he could manage only a hoarse croak. Then he darted to his cupboard, took out some yellow-golden liquid, tore a whip off the wall, and screamed:

"You shall be turned into a mangy dog, and I will beat you until you cannot howl any more."

So saying, he sprinkled Wendelin with the contents of the bottle, and murmured a few accompanying words. But great was his dismay when Wendelin stood there quietly smiling, and no change whatsoever took place in him. The wizard began to tremble, he stared at the boy as at an incomprehensible miracle. Then he suddenly sank to his knees and cried: "He has the ring! He has the ring!" Now he crawled to Wendelin, clasped him round the knees, and begged and besought him to give him the ring. He overwhelmed him with flattery and promises. Then he ran off, and came back with one bag of gold after the other. He emptied out a heap of it on to the floor, where it flashed and glittered in the sunlight, and then he fetched all the remaining valuables he possessed, and added them to the pile. He would have given all this to Wendelin in return for the ring.

Then the boy realised how valuable this possession was, and he pushed the pleading wizard away from him, took his hat, and went out of the door.

5 *The End*

Wendelin left the town and wandered on till he reached the nearest wood. There, well hidden in the heavy shadows of a plantation of young fir-trees, he stuck the ring on his finger and, because he felt rather nervous, he shut his eyes before turning it round not once but four times. Now he dared not open his eyes, but listened, instead, for any sound. But the only thing he noticed was the perfume of freshly turned soil. From one side, a current of air blew on him: from the other, he felt a warm glow like the flame of an open fire: and in the background he could hear the sort of trickling and gurgling that spring-water makes. At last he decided to open his eyes, and saw before him four well-dressed young men, none of whom were in the least bit frightening or repulsive. One was dressed in dark brown material embroidered with brightly coloured flowers, and he wore a green cap. Another wore garments the colour of fire, and his blackish hat had a grey feather which waved in the lightest breath of wind. The third wore sea-green silk, and his head was covered by a flossy cap, crisp as sea-foam, while the fourth went about in sky-blue, and wore a glittering golden cap upon his shining yellow hair. All four stood humbly there in silent anticipation, as though before their lord and master. Wendelin did not hesitate long. He commanded that a beautiful horse, an expensive suit of clothes, a well-filled valise and a large bag full of gold pieces be brought to him, dressed himself with the assistance of these obedient servants, and rode out into the world in high good humour. And thus he travelled through many towns and countries, everywhere warmly welcomed and regretfully dismissed, because he distributed the gold with generosity. The treasures of the earth, the pearls of the ocean, the power of fire, were all at his disposal, and whatever his heart desired was quickly brought from the far corners of the globe by the speedy spirits of the air.

But he did not forget what the clever magpie had told him. After he had travelled the world for ten months, he came to a lovely spot which pleased him greatly. There he bought a large piece of land and built a splendid castle beside a lake and beautifully situated between two huge forests. With the help of the spirits, it was done in no time, and there was nothing in the whole land to compare with it. On the day on which it was completed exactly a year had passed since he had left the wizard, and on the anniversary of that event, he was sitting at an open window through which one could look out over the blue lake to the green sea of tree-tops in the far distance. Wendelin played with the ring, drew it from his finger, and let the gold-coloured jewel which ornamented it flash in the sunlight. Suddenly there was the sound of wings, and the magpie Shackerack landed on the window-sill, took the ring from his hand, flew off, and was soon out of sight between the forest tree-tops.

Later, Wendelin married a beautiful girl; his descendants are still flourishing today.

On New Year's Eve in the year Wendelin left Angleburg, a terrible noise had broken out towards midnight in Mr Sugarman's house. A fiery glow was seen in the windows, and some people said that they had seen two shapes fighting each other within. Suddenly it became pitch-dark, and at that instant, a flaming thing with a long, glowing tail shot out of the chimney into the sky. The next morning, a few brave people forced an entry into the house, and there lay Mr Sugarman on the sofa; he was quite blue in the face, and his neck was broken. Among his possessions was a great chest filled with gold and many valuables: but to the great astonishment of the town-folk, most of the cupboards and drawers were filled with sand and earth.

The Magic Inkstand

ONCE THERE WAS a poor student who lived all alone in a big town and had no one in the world to care for him. One summer's day he was walking along a street at dusk when he met a strange-looking man with a dog-cart – that is to say, a little cart with a dog between its shafts pulling it along. The man was small and bent, and he wore a long grey coat with big pockets and a large, broad-brimmed hat was set so low upon his head that one could hardly see his small face with its grey beard and deep-set black eyes. With his long overcoat buttoned down the front and his big black hat, he somewhat resembled a giant mushroom.

The man left the cart near the curb while he went from house to house collecting rags and bones and any old junk that people didn't want any more. Hans had just seen him disappear into one of the houses when a street-urchin started to tease the poor dog, who could not defend himself because he was harnessed between the shafts. He growled and barked and snapped at the stick the boy was holding, but he couldn't reach him to give him the bite he so richly deserved. Hans grew very angry when he saw this, and he crossed the street, snatched the stick away from the boy and gave him a good beating with it so that he yelled with pain. By this time, the old man had come back, and told Hans to stop. "Let the boy go," he said: "he should have learned his lesson by now." So Hans let go of the howling boy, who ran off, while Hans stroked and patted the dog. The rag-and-bone man gave the student a friendly look, pressed his hand, and said: "I won't forget your good deed. Come, Bello . . ." And the cart rolled off.

Summer passed, autumn came, and then the first snow fell and it was nearly Christmas time, but Hans had not run into the old man again. On Christmas Eve, he was wandering through the town, and the lighted shops busy with last-minute customers made him feel lonelier than ever. He had just turned into a dark alley-way to escape from the festive atmosphere when suddenly someone called out to him, and there was the old man standing in the doorway of a shabby old house.

"Come in," said the man, "I am going to be your Father Christmas tonight." He led him into a small, warm room. A lamp burned on the table beside an open Bible. The walls were covered in shelves on which all kinds of things were stacked – some useful, and some just junk. There were books and vases, cooking utensils and old paintings, broken pots and all the sort of stuff that tramps collect.

The old man sat down at the table and put on a large pair of horn-rimmed spectacles. Then he read the Christmas story aloud to Hans out of the Bible. The student listened thoughtfully, while Bello pricked his ears and looked at his master as though he understood every word. The old man's trembling voice rose towards the end as he repeated the words of the angels: "Glory be to God in the highest and on earth peace – good will towards men!" Then he rummaged about in a cupboard and produced a bottle of wine and a large cake.

"Now we will celebrate Christmas," he said, "and eat

cake and drink wine. Everybody is eating cake tonight, and Bello is going to have some too, aren't you, Bello?"

He poured wine into two sparkling crystal glasses and told Hans to drink up. How fragrant it was! The blood coursed through his veins like fire; the wine seemed to melt in his mouth so that he felt as though he were swallowing pure spirit. How different the poor old tramp's room looked to him now! Valuable vases and crystal-ware shone down from the shelves where before he had seen only a lot of old, broken pots. Mysterious rustlings and scufflings could be heard in dark corners; sometimes he thought he saw a bearded dwarf's head pop up from behind one of the big books or peep out of a vase. But when he looked more closely, he could not discern anything out of the ordinary. Meanwhile the old man had put on a coloured dressing-gown and a tall, pointed cap, so that he looked like a magician.

"Now we are going to look at pictures," he said, and laid a big book on the table. He opened it, and touched the illustrations with a little stick. It must have been a magic wand, for lo and behold, they came alive!

How everything lived and moved! They were looking at a Christmas fair. There were brightly lit stalls stacked with toys. People were walking round them laden with parcels. At one stall there were a lot of Christmas trees. A poor woman had bought a small tree. Her two children were holding on to her skirts, smiling so happily. Now they were each given a tree as well. Hans thought he could hear the voices of the crowd and the plaintive note of a barrel-organ. Surely this was no picture. Everything in it seemed so alive and real!

"Turn over!" said the old man, and Hans thought he glimpsed a dwarf popping out from beneath the page, quickly turning it over, and then vanishing as quickly as he had appeared.

A storm at sea. How the water surged and foamed! A ship was riding the waves and they broke over her decks. It was Christmas Eve at sea. Sailors were sitting on the leeward side, sheltered from wind and waves; they were talking and smoking their pipes. The cabin-boy stood with one arm round the mast, careless of the storm; his brown cheeks were wet with salt tears. For his brothers and sisters were dancing round their candle-lit tree at that very moment, while he was out on the great, wild ocean, too young to be away from home at Christmas time.

And so on to the next page.

A brightly lit Christmas tree stood on the table. Students sat all around it drinking punch: they were celebrating Christmas in their own way. A lot of silly things were hanging on the tree: children's whistles, string puppets and funny dolls with big heads. They had unwrapped all their parcels from home. Letters and presents lay about among nuts, dates and crackers.

One of the students had a piece of Christmas cake in his hand and was just about to take a bite out of it. Another was sitting a little way away from the others; he was holding a home-made embroidered pocket-book and secretly kissing it. And Hans thought he could hear happy laughter and the clinking of glasses.

And so, one after another, the pages were turned over, and Hans sat and looked and forgot where he was and laughed and cried with pleasure at all that he saw.

When the book was finished, the pages rustled and spread themselves out. Green pine-twigs sprouted from them and grew ever taller with lights sparkling between them until, when Hans looked up, he saw that a huge Christmas tree covered with candles had grown out of the pages

of the book until it filled the room. The ceiling had moved upwards and the walls outwards to make room for it, and the floor was covered with sweet-smelling flowers.

Hans was alone amid all this glory when the branches of the tree parted and a beautiful girl stepped out. She wore a white dress and had a wreath of pine-twigs in her hair. She took Hans by the hand, and they climbed up the tree together as though it were a ladder. In the distance Hans kept hearing an organ playing and voices singing as they do in church. They climbed higher and higher: now and then he caught a glimpse of the night-sky through the branches and a myriad shining stars.

Suddenly they were looking down from a great height at the whole town spread below them. The houses were brightly lit, and the sound of happy voices reached their ears. "Look up!" said the girl.

There was a white cloud high above their heads that suddenly seemed to open like a doorway into Heaven itself. Hans could see angels dressed all in white holding palm-branches in their hands, and hear them singing:

"Glory be to God in the highest and on earth peace – good will towards men!"

"It is high time you went home now," growled the old tramp's voice in his ear. "It is nearly midnight." And there he was, sitting at the table, and everything looking quite ordinary. The book had disappeared, and the old man was rummaging in a drawer.

"Did you enjoy your nap?" he said.

"Have I been dreaming then?" asked Hans in confusion.

"Go to bed: you are tired," said the old man, avoiding the question. "And here is a little present for you, which should come in useful to a diligent student." So saying, he pressed an old, curiously fashioned inkstand into his hand

and pushed him out of the door. And as Hans walked home through the gas-lit streets, he felt as though he had dreamed the whole thing. Yet the inkstand he held in his hands was real enough.

When Hans woke up rather late next morning, he still believed that the experiences of the previous evening had been a dream; but then he saw the inkstand that the old man had given him standing on the table where he had put it the night before. And all the magic pictures he had taken part in became a reality.

He got up and looked out of the window. Snow had fallen during the night. The white roof-tops sparkled in the sunshine, the sky was blue, sparrows twittered in the nearby trees and the air was full of bells chiming for Christmas Day.

In the evening, Hans sat alone at the table in his little room. He had put a white sheet of paper in front of him, and was thoughtfully contemplating the inkstand. It was beautifully made of metal, and consisted of a sandbox – for in those days there was no blotting-paper and fine sand was sprinkled on the ink to dry it – and a tray to put pens and pen-nibs in, as well as the ink-pot itself. The stand was composed of a fine metal creeper all twisted in and out and covered with copper-coloured leaves and flowers. In between these sat delicately wrought lizards, beetles and butterflies. Here and there, little bearded dwarfs peeped through the tendrils, and some of the flowers had tiny elves sitting in them. In the centre of the stand, where the leaves formed a small grotto, there sat a tiny girl with a crown on her head and a wand in her hand; it was all so finely and delicately made that Hans could not take his eyes from it.

All at once, he felt that he must write something.

As soon as he dipped the pen in the ink, he felt a little shock which was enough to make his fingers twitch, and he was certain that he could see one of the dwarfs nodding to him. From that moment on, the whole inkstand came alive. The creeper started to grow before his very eyes and spread itself right over the table, and red, white and blue flowers appeared between the leaves, while dwarfs popped in and out of its tendrils. Each flower, as it opened, contained a little elf which flew out and joined in a game with some brightly coloured butterflies. Big, shiny beetles and glittering lizards slipped through the tangle of intertwined stalks and flowers.

Then Hans heard some gay music, and a procession of bearded dwarfs appeared. The band came first, marching along with golden trumpets, drums and flutes. It was followed by dwarfs wearing shining gold armour and mounted on enormous stag-beetles. They carried tiny lances in their hands, and it was comical to see how gravely they sat astride their brown steeds, and to watch the fat beetles trying to make their six legs march in time to the music. A small army of elves then appeared, wearing pointed hats and carrying sharp blades of grass at the ready. But they got in a bit of a muddle because elves are too airy-fairy to march in line.

Now the ringing of silver bells was followed by a number of little elfin-girls: each danced along with a harebell on a swaying stalk in her hand. Twelve elves came after them carrying a throne made of interwoven flowers, and on it sat a little tiny girl with a golden crown on her head and a wand in her hand. Grey-bearded dwarfs marched on either side of her; they wore silver breastplates and carried spears. Above and behind the throne, the air was full of elves riding magnificent butterflies. Then came some more elves, and the rearguard was formed by a body of black-bearded dwarfs mounted on swift lizards: they wore turbans on their heads and carried curved swords.

When the throne had been set down in the midst of this colourful gathering, the trumpets sounded three times, and all the dwarfs and elves shouted: "Hurrah!" as loudly as they could. Then the girl rose from her throne, bowed three times to Hans and said:

"My lord and master, will you allow me and my people to hold a festival here tonight?"

"Who are you?" asked Hans, quite confused by all the amazing things he had just seen.

"I am the Fairy-Tale," said the girl, "and I am at your pen's command."

So Hans nodded his head, for he did not know what to say.

Then all the little people formed a semi-circle. The elves and dwarfs sat on the ground and behind and above them the little elfin-girls: the Queen sat in the middle. The stag-beetles were put out to graze in the moss, and the butterflies were tethered to the flowers with cobwebs so that they could sip nectar while they rested.

Then the festival began with a sort of fairy circus.

Elves walked the tightrope on tightly-stretched spider-threads; little elf-girls stood and cleverly kept their balance on rolling dewdrops; a fat dwarf stuck a tall candle in his belt and allowed elves to climb up it and the smallest one stood on his head at the top. Everyone clapped this brilliant stunt and cried: "Bravo!"

After this, an aerial battle took place. Elves mounted on their swiftest butterflies pretended to fight one another above the arena.

Then came the Dwarf Dance. They came waddling in accompanied by very funny music of their own; they carried picks over their shoulders and little blue lights on their heads – like miners in olden times. Each had a precious or semi-precious stone in his hand. They formed a circle, hopped into the middle, and laid the stones in a heap. After which they danced about, leaping in the most comical manner, stamping their feet and singing in time to the music in their gruff voices:

"Little dwarfs deep underground
must dig and labour day and night
till the jewels which abound
in the earth are brought to light.
Little dwarfs beneath the hill –
never resting – never still –
always digging with a will.
Pick-a-hoe – here we go . . ."

And as they jumped and stamped they gradually began to sink into the ground. Soon only their bearded faces were visible. Then they disappeared altogether, and only the blue flames flickered at the spot where they had vanished. Once more their voices could be heard echoing faintly from underground:

"never resting, never still –
always digging with a will.
Pick-a-hoe – here we go . . ."

Then there was silence and the little flames went out.

Now it was the turn of the elves. To a much lighter musical accompaniment, they danced and flew about the Queen holding their ringing harebells and singing:

"Come and join our airy flight!
Elfin dancers in the night.
Come and float and laugh and play
till the dawning of the day!"

And as Hans looked at the moving throng it seemed to become more and more indistinct; the little dancing figures seemed to be veiled in mist, and their song came to him as though from a great distance:

"Come and join our airy flight!
Elfin dancers in the night . . ."

Then all was still, and it was as though a curtain fell over Hans's eyes, and he saw no more.

When he opened his eyes again it was morning and he was lying in his bed. The clock on the nearby church-tower struck eight. He rubbed his forehead, sat up in bed and looked over at the inkstand. It was on the table looking no different than usual.

When he got up and went over to the table, he was astonished to see that the whole sheet of paper he had put before him the night before was closely covered with his own handwriting. When he began to read what was written there, he found that it was an exact description of the elfin festival. Now the poor student realised what a valuable present the old man had given him. So he set off at once to visit him and to thank him for his gift. But when he reached the street where he had found him on Christmas Eve, he could not find the house in which he lived, search as he might. And indeed he never did see the old rag-and-bone man again.

But on many an evening to come, he would put the

inkstand on the table, place a sheet of paper before it, take the pen in his hand, and dip it in the ink. As soon as he did so, another marvellous fairy-story would come into being.

The children who lived in the same house as Hans were very lucky, because they could go to his room and sit around him when darkness fell, and he would tell them all these wonderful stories. I suppose you would like to hear them too, wouldn't you?

But surely you must realise that you already know them, that is, provided you have read this book carefully all through. Because these stories, all full of colour and movement and enchantment as they are, all came out of the Magic Inkstand.